Never S

Keelan LaForge

ISBN: 9798812276515

Copyright[1] © 2022 Keelan LaForge

Credits for Cover – james@goonwrite.com
Printed in Belfast, United Kingdom.
Publisher – Independently Published

Chapter One

All things considered - I was happy to be human. It's a privileged position to occupy in our world. When I think about being a cat or dog – the comfort might be pleasant if you found yourself in a happy household, but if you struck it unlucky, things could get grim. I could have ended up inside any creature's body on Earth, but I ended up embodying the human form. Of course, there are downsides to being human. In my experience, most people spend a large chunk of their lives complaining about something. There are big problems and small problems. There are worries and bad feelings. Maybe if I'd been a monkey, my existence could have been easier, but the work feels like a fair pay off for all the opportunities I had.

I've never been a needlessly cruel person – no more than the average person. I felt like I had a good heart. I was brought up to believe that people with good, godly hearts always went to heaven. In a predominantly Christian country, we had that drilled into us from an early age. Our afterlife experience depended entirely upon our comportment in our lives. I was taken to church every Sunday, fed through the Sunday school system along with all the other children. I had the same lessons taught to me so many times they became branded on my brain. It was like I couldn't disassociate myself from them and we were forever linked. My parents liked when someone else taught you the same story from a slightly different angle. It kept it interesting, they thought, but there was always the same ending. With Christianity, everything seems simple – if you're willing to be good.

I was a happy child. I know that there were people less fortunate. I had chores and things I didn't want to do, but I never had to do things I couldn't stand to do – things that would have put me in a position of moral disquietude. I know now that that was a gift. It's strange to be able to see back into that time in my life like I'm looking through a window. I can touch the glass, but I can never get the attention of the person behind it ever again. I can see her skipping in the outhouse on a wet day through the cobwebs collected on the inside of the windowpane. I can hear the bluebottle beating against the window, desperate to make its final exit before the eight-legged fiend makes its return to its web for dinner. That wasn't the focal point of the memory, but now it stands out to me. I was vaguely aware of it at the age of seven, but I was occupied with my skipping practice. My best friend could skip, and I was determined to develop the same skill she had, however long it took me. I stayed there all afternoon, failing but trying again and again. I was proud of myself when I managed to count twenty rounds of the rope at a time. It felt like a big achievement – maybe even bigger than anything I accomplished as an adult. I can still see my golden hair bouncing with each bound I took. I can hear the rope slicing through the air and slapping off the ground. It doesn't feel far away, but it's an era that's distant and finished forever.

When I got older, I was afraid to leave home. I was very attached to my parents. They'd been so kind to me for so many years that I was afraid if I left, I'd find everyone else cold by comparison. I'd lived in a beautiful little world but listening to the news on the wireless with my parents had revealed to me just how sad things could be on the outside. I was protected but I wasn't ignorant either. I didn't feel like I was ever owed happiness.

I left my family home at the age of eighteen to move to the nearest city in search of work. Women didn't frequently attend university then. It was still frowned upon. I was bright, but I didn't think I would have had the brains for it, even if I'd had the opportunity to go. I thought I was better suited to something gentler.

I got a job working in a laundromat/clothing alterations shop. I'd learnt to sew as a child, and I was happy to use my busy hands. They were always engaged in whatever they were doing, even if my mind wondered elsewhere. I would dream about the things that could be improved upon – like everyone does. While I worked, I got time to think about all the things I could have done instead. I wasn't unhappy with my lot in life. I think I was happy to sit there and have the chance to daydream all day. I had the money to pay for a room and I had reasonable freedom for a woman at that time. I could come and go as I pleased, and so long as I was managing to live and enjoying myself, my parents didn't ask any questions. I realised later just how fortunate I was in that way. At the time, I didn't know a different way.

We always had plenty of custom in that little shop. It was situated on the corner of a row of houses in a residential area. There were regulars that called in to get their coats laundered and any items they needed altered. I was lucky to often be seated at the sewing machine beside the window. There was nothing remarkable outside, but I just liked watching the sky and whatever passing birds I caught a glimpse of. In the summer, we opened the windows to let some clean air in. It was a small shop and it quickly got stuffy inside. When it did, the owner opened all the windows at once. The cool currents gave us great relief, but then the insects descended upon us. We always seemed to have a bluebottle nonsensically butting the window. It never seemed to understand that there was an available opening. The frantic buzzing it made was irritating. Eventually, I'd get fed up with it and swat it with a rolled-up newspaper. The carcasses went into the bin with the rest of the rubbish. The flies were probably the dirtiest things in there. Even though they were living beings, I never saw them as such. They were like little wind-up creatures that ran out of steam when their time was up. Natural death or not, they only had a short life span anyway. It was inconsequential compared with anything else.

I worked with one lady that I got on particularly well with. She had a radical way of looking at the world and I loved her spirit. She was one of those people that you knew had had a rough life, but she chose to overlook it. That inspired me. I'd never had any kind of hardship in mine, but she didn't seem to respect me less for it. She was called Emily and she always made me laugh. We didn't even have a radio in work, so it was good to have someone fun to talk to. She was big on women's rights. At the time, it felt like we had few of them. She said we were treated like second class citizens, but no one seemed to have time to protest it, much less notice it. I can't recall ever seeing a demonstration like the ones in America I'd later see on the news. We'd hear whispers about things like that taking place thousands of miles away, but nothing like it close to home.

She didn't put up with being talked down to by any men, even if she was doing their laundry. It was inspiring to see someone so full of feistiness when so many others were complacent. I looked forward to seeing her more and more each day. It felt like we were friends on a different, special kind of level. We lived in each other's pockets too. Our workplace was so small, if we hadn't got along, it would have proven very difficult. I think my upbringing enabled me to get on well with most people I met. That was one of the benefits of living with parents that always thought the best of everyone.

I had always liked the name Emily. I suppose it started with reading Emily Dickenson's poetry. My mother always had plenty of poetry books lying around and she was my favourite. I had read them so many times that each poem had taken on a personal meaning for me. It was like they'd been composed especially for my enjoyment. So, I was fond of the name Emily before we were introduced. People always assume if you work with your hands that you don't employ your mind much. But that isn't true at all. I still enjoyed learning in my free time, and Emily wanted to learn with me. She taught me so much through the stories she told and retold about her difficult upbringing. No matter how heavy and sad the anecdotes got, she still always managed to make me laugh.

Our manager was a simple lady. She was bossy and perfectionistic; I suppose she was perfect for the role. She always checked everything over thoroughly before we returned it to the customer. Her eye caught details everyone else's missed. She was an asset to the business, but she didn't bring a great deal of personality to the place. Maybe that encouraged Emily and me to get closer too.

For all her bravado, I remember noticing Emily's tender heart when I swatted a fly once. I hit it hard with the newspaper and it fell to the windowsill. It lay there sadly – upside-down and lifeless. Emily had gasped. "Oh, please don't kill it."

"It's too late."

"It wasn't doing any harm."

"They're dirty – and annoying."

"Maybe they think that about us. Maybe in their little world, they believe we are the intruders."

I thought it was a funny personality quirk of hers – the fact she cared so much about the littlest things. It was endearing, even though she flinched any time you wafted a fly away.

I was usually sitting sewing alongside Emily. We had a sewing machine each. They were the old fashioned heavy, steel kind and they were always cold to the touch. Sometimes Emily would warm my hand up underneath the table. Her touch was reassuring. It reminded me that I wasn't just alone with my machine – living a robotic type of existence. I was using my hands to create beautiful masterpieces – whether anyone else acknowledged them as such or not. We were doing something worthwhile in that little studio. In the absence of the incessant buzzing, the moments we spent there could almost be considered perfect.

Chapter Two

Trying to reconcile what I was doing with my Christian upbringing wasn't easy. It ran against everything I'd been taught. My parents didn't mind what I did. I knew it was impossible to disappoint them as an adult. But it felt possible to disappoint society. No one was living like we were then. In Northern Ireland, such things were unspeakable, never mind something you could promote in public places.

Emily and I first spent time together outside work on a day when we'd been alone for the workday. Ann, the manager, wasn't in that day. She had a bad case of tonsillitis and she'd asked us to hold down the fort until she got better. She had bouts of it every year. They were talking about removing her tonsils, but she was reluctant to go ahead with it. For how forthcoming and decisive Ann was, she was fearful when it came to her health.

Emily and I started our workday as usual. She wasn't sitting beside me because she was taking care of customers and ironing. I noticed her absence as I sat behind my machine. It felt like it wasn't working smoothly that day. The bobbin ran out and I kept having to change colours. It wasn't the mindless kind of work I wanted to do. I was always thinking ahead of what I was doing, trying to pre-empt each upcoming change. I kept getting the thread tangled and having to rethread the needle. I felt tension in the air, but I couldn't have identified why it was – not consciously at least.

Emily and I didn't get a chance to say more than two words to each other. I could suddenly see how much Ann's presence had helped our friendship to flourish. She took care of the admin, the customer conversation, and the laundered clothes. We were a team of three, but Emily and I were somehow more bonded to one another.

After work that day, Emily pulled the shutters down before she counted the day's intake. We had made more money than we usually did. I knew that Ann would be pleased. I hoped she'd return to work soon though. She was the cog that made the whole machine run smoothly.

When I was finishing sewing my last item of the day and Emily had finished counting the money, she crossed the room in my direction and gave me a hug.

"You look like you need one," she said, smiling.

I didn't know if she really believed that or if she was just looking for an excuse to touch me. I felt her hand on top of mine, pressing down on it with meaning. Her face was so clean it was shiny. We didn't wear make-up. I didn't know anyone that did then. It wasn't readily available or encouraged. It was a less superficial time. I knew there was nothing superficial about my connection with Emily either.

Her wavy brown hair was always tied up in a tight bun. One strand of hair had freed itself and it fell against her cheek. It looked completely beautiful to me. I wrestled with that feeling, wondering why on Earth I was having it. Was she objectively or subjectively beautiful? That was the question whose answer threatened my sense of self.

Emily took care of locking up. She knew the routine, and so did I. I wanted to finish working on the last piece I had started. I never left a day's work unfinished. If I began to sew an item of clothing, it had to be complete before I could leave it. But Emily distracted me from it. She was being perfectly ordinary – walking around, checking the light switches, pulling the windows closed, wafting whatever insects had made a frenzied entrance in the last of the daylight, back outside with a towel. She slammed the windows shut behind them, but she let them out gently first. I liked that about her, even though I didn't see the point in it.

She walked past me, away from the window and landed in my lap. I was taken aback, even though I should have seen it coming. I felt strange stirrings inside me, but I hadn't recognised what they were. I thought we were just close friends, but Emily wanted more. I didn't know how to react to it. I felt like it was wrong to behave that way. It ran against everything religious I'd seen up to that point. I didn't want to feel frowned upon by other Christians. Even though I knew my parents would accept me no matter what, it felt like a big decision to make – that small gesture of acceptance.

I wrapped my arms around Emily and kissed her. The windows were little black squares without curtains. No one had ever spent time there at night, so there was no need for us to have them. But I was suddenly worried that someone might pass one and look in at us. I turned my back to the window, so what we were doing was less visible. I had never kissed anyone before – man nor woman. Her lips were supple and her pressure, gentle. She was beautiful in the dim light. I didn't want to think that, but I did. I had never thought of myself as being attracted to women. Maybe I still wasn't – maybe it was just specific to her.

We kissed slowly and lengthily. She ran her fingers through my hair, combing it and massaging my head. Those were the days long before CCTV, so we didn't have to worry about being caught on camera – just about being caught in person. I hoped we would be safe where we were situated. That particular street was never busy once night had descended on it.

The dynamic between myself and Emily had forever changed. I didn't know how to feel about it. We would continue to see each other every day, knowing what had happened. I didn't know yet what it meant. Would it be a one-off occurrence, never mentioned again, or the establishment of something permanent between us? There was a lone spider weaving a web on the wooden window frame. The web glistened in the low lighting, and I could almost see the beauty in its creation. But I couldn't stand spiders either – even if they took on the job of killing the flies for us. I didn't like the thought of their legs tickling my skin as they marched uninvited across my body. I grabbed a piece of paper and crushed the spider in it. I let the web hang there. It was like a home without a person to care for it.

"You shouldn't have done that," said Emily, whispering into my mouth between kisses.

"Why are you so protective of insects?"

"I love all living things."

"They're not really living things though – they are just a nuisance."

"I guess it all depends on your perspective," said Emily.

She had grown up on a homestead in the countryside – a place that depended on only nature to feed them and to thrive. She saw each little insect as something valuable. I couldn't change my attitude to match hers. I was too jumpy around them. They had the potential to harm in ways we couldn't even conceive of. Maybe they'd fill us with their poison or germs, maybe we'd discover an unknown allergy to them when it was too late to act. I didn't like the movement of them either. Other creatures had a charm to their walks and acrobatics, but not insects. I could appreciate the flutter of a butterfly. But anything else crept along in a way that made the hairs on my body stand up straight.

After work, we left together. Emily was living in a boarding room too. We all were, as single, working women. It was like punishment for our resistance to male dominance. We had to sacrifice all comfort for our right to live independently. Emily's room was almost identical to my own. Everything in it was a shade of beige – faded things that once might have clung onto colour. They were washed out – probably from years of over-washing between tenants. She had a single bed that didn't look very sturdy. It was very lumpy, and it bulged under the covers. There was a simple blanket placed on top of the sheets. It had a grainy texture to it that reminded me of hospital beds and sickness. There were frayed curtains framing the window and cracked paint on the walls. Beside the bed, stood a little table with an oil lamp on it. Emily lit it with a match, and it glowed with a romantic lustre.

I stood in the doorway, a little awkwardly, waiting for Emily to tell me where to sit. There was only one chair in the room, and it was covered in her clothes. In the dark it almost would have looked like a person – someone to keep her company in the loneliness. There was a fireplace in the room, but it wasn't lit. It probably never was. Coal was a luxury we weren't treated to. The proprietor of the building occupied a little office downstairs. She was stern and sharp when we came in. I knew she didn't like the look of me, but she hadn't refused me as a visitor. I was glad I'd passed by her watchful gaze. I'd expected our meeting to be intercepted at the door. But people didn't think of things in that way. Two women together meant something different then – sisterhood, seamstress workmates, two women ready to repair a ripped curtain together, to attend to the needs of others together - not to their own.

Emily closed the door behind me and looked at me with humour in her eyes. "Aren't you staying?" she asked.

"I don't like to intrude."

"You sit next to me every day. I'm used to the intrusion," she smiled.

Then she reached out and touched my hair and caressed it lightly, twirling it around her finger and releasing it, adjusting the placement of it to where she wanted it to sit. She kissed me lengthily and I made an involuntary noise into her mouth. She laughed at me, in an affectionate way rather than one of mockery.

We lay down on the bed together, hugging each other tightly. It didn't feel strange at all, even though I knew it should have felt strange. I had no point of comparison. I had never kissed anyone before – not even a man. I hadn't given much thought to the topic either. It didn't feel like it was something pertinent in my life. I was focussed on work and making my way in the world, on enjoying my already established relationships with family and on thinking out my future goals. Love wasn't on the agenda. But I wondered if that was what it was? How could I know the difference between love and lust at such a young age? They felt like one and the same to me.

Emily held me tightly in an embrace. I could feel her breath on the back of my ear, and it was comforting. She wanted to be near me, and I never stopped to question whether I should allow it. It felt natural to me, even though everyone in the community would have disputed how natural it really was. I couldn't think of one example of a similar situation. But it didn't matter because it felt like something that happened organically. We never had to stop and consider it or hit the pause button.

A fly landed on my nose, and I brushed it away. I seemed to be plagued by my least favourite creatures – followed around everywhere I went in life, even when I was meant to be somewhat protected from them indoors.

"Don't worry," said Emily. "I can feel you tensing up, but it won't do anything to you."

All the insects of the earth were nothing but irritations to me. I didn't know how she so wholeheartedly accepted everything. It was beautiful to me. She was beautiful to me.

Chapter Three

I was working on a dress that needed hemmed. It was an easy job, and I was glad of the thinking time it afforded me. Emily wasn't in work that day; she had caught a bad cold the day before and had agreed with Ann to stay at home for a day to sleep it off. Without her there, the atmosphere was entirely different. I felt relieved in a way to be separated from each other for a short time. It had all been happening very thick and fast. But I missed her too – more than I imagined I could in such a short period. Our employer still had no inkling about what was happening between us, and we planned to keep it that way. Emily said she wasn't ashamed of me, that she'd gladly announce me from the rooftops, but we wanted to keep our jobs too, and you never could tell who might be the most judgemental and punitive. We were doing something new. Well, it felt like that anyway.

I had gone to stay with my parents at the weekend. Sometimes I just felt the desperate need to get out of the boarding room. The walls were closing in on me. I was sharing all the facilities with strangers. That boxed in room was the only patch of land I had to myself. It was dirty and it was hard to clean it. I had to borrow the dustpan and brush when no one else was using it. There were some cleaning supplies held downstairs in the airing cupboard, but other tenants often took them into their locked rooms and forgot to return them. I didn't have the spare cash to buy such things for myself. Between paying for my room and food, I only had pennies to spare at the end of the week. At that time, there was nothing much to do anyway. Had I wanted to spend money, it would have been much harder to find ways in which to do it. The world as I left it was a much different, less money-orientated place. You could render yourself bankrupt in a matter of minutes. I never worried about saving money then. There was no defined future I had to save for. The idea of buying my own house was a ridiculous one to consider. I never could have done it, so it was ruled right out.

My parents were as happy as ever to see me. We hadn't seen each other in weeks. That was the longest period of separation we had ever had. I was only miles away from them, but we didn't use public transport then for unnecessary trips. Going home was a big expenditure. We made the most of every moment. I chose not to mention Emily to my parents. I wasn't afraid of their judgement; I was afraid that what we had mightn't last. I didn't know exactly what it was or how to define it.

My dad was so happy to see me that he got tearful. I thought that was very progressive for a man from his generation. He'd lived through two wars, when people were stoic and discouraged from crying. But he was never shy about showing his feelings.

"Betsy," he said, taking my hand and squeezing it like we hadn't seen each other in years.

It felt like that was the case. My mother was making a big dinner celebration. My parents lived by the Bible in everything they did, but they didn't impose rigid rules on others. They didn't believe in being hard on me. I was thankful for that. It made me feel like one day, I might be able to reveal to them the secret of who I really was. There was untapped potential inside me – not so much with respect to work or standardised success. But I felt there was so much to discover that even I didn't yet know about. I was still pliable and able to be moulded and remoulded into something new.

My mum served us a huge chicken dinner. The roast bird was as big as a turkey feast at Christmas. The potatoes and vegetables were abundant. I tasted my mum's gravy and realised how much I had missed it without consciously thinking about it. It was one of those barely noticed daily details that make up who you are as a person. My childhood was drenched in that gravy, the flavour of it following me through adolescence and into adulthood.

We ate voraciously. It felt like I hadn't been fed in weeks – not by food at least. I didn't have my own kitchen and there was just a scullery in the building I lived in. I bought cheap and easy things to make, like eggs, ham and bread. It was an indescribable comfort to have a homecooked meal for a change.

Sleeping in my bed that night was as much of a reward. It wasn't lumpy. I had a very comfortable mattress that yielded to the weight added to it, becoming like a personalised pillow to a tired form. The curtains succeeded in keeping the light out in the morning. I hadn't got up in daylight for a long time. I realised that then. I'd been plodding off to work when it was as dark as midnight, nocturnal animals still rustling in the small patches of vegetation the city had.

Getting comfortable made me consider not returning to the city, but I knew I had to make my own way too. And Emily would be waiting for me, impatiently, I imagined. She hadn't seemed delighted by the prospect of us being separated. She'd smiled and wished me well, but I could see the sadness in her eyes too. That made me think she loved me and that it wasn't just a meaningless moment in her life. Even though I had every comfort in my parents' house, I realised just how happy I was, lying in a broken bed with her, feeling her body heat against my own.

I fell into a heavy slumber and dreamt vividly of her. I had only ever seen her fully clothed, but in my dream, she wasn't, and our bodies melded together like something in the spiritual world. It didn't feel sinful, even though the teachings I knew so well told me it must have been. But they were just thoughts, circling in my sleeping mind. They were yet to become concrete realities – ones that were decisions I'd made about my life.

My parents' house was more rural than where I lived, but it wasn't deep in the countryside either. We weren't plagued by bugs, but they did make an appearance. No matter where I went to, it felt like I could never fully escape them. I'd killed a spider in my boarding room that week. I'd momentarily felt bad about it. Its spindly legs had been crushed, along with the rest of it. Vivacious only moments before, I had decided to put a stop to that. I'd been worried about it walking on me whilst I slept. I'd never met someone with such a strong aversion to bugs before. I knew that they weren't popular with plenty of people, but I had a special fear of even the most benign little buggies.

I didn't outstay my welcome at my folks' house – not that I felt I could. I didn't want to unwind too much. I was in pursuit of my independence, and I had to keep it up. I needed to please my employer too, or I wouldn't advance in the working world. I didn't make much money at all. I made a few pounds a week. It was enough to buy basic food and I didn't have a use for the remainder of it. Once I paid my board and lighting, I gave the rest to the nearest church. I didn't ever set foot in it, but they had a donations box on a post outside. I passed it every day on my walk to work. I wanted to support whatever good works they were doing. I knew if they knew what I'd allowed to happen in my free time, they wouldn't have wanted my tainted money, but I still gladly gave it. I still felt attached to my faith in God, even if I wasn't intentionally practising it.

I needed new shoes, but I didn't have the funds to get them. I'd managed to scrape together enough to get them reheeled after work. I'd had to wait in the shop while the man did them. I didn't have a spare pair to wear home. Most didn't then. Everything was more used and more appreciated. "One of a kind" meant something.

When I saw Emily again, I felt a strong surge of passion. I realised I'd missed her like I'd lost a valuable part of myself. She came to my room to meet me on the night she knew I was back. She stayed in my bed, and we talked in the dark for hours.

"What did you dream of doing when you were a child?" I asked her.

"I never had the same dreams as other girls in school. They wanted husbands and beautiful houses and a fairytale wedding. I wanted to do my own thing and to meet someone with flowing hair like yours," she said.

"Did you think you were a lesbian?" I asked.

"I knew I was before I knew there was a name for it. I just knew men didn't appeal to me. What about you?"

"I thought I was asexual before I met you. I just never had any romantic interest in anyone."

"Are you glad to be proven wrong?"

"It wasn't something I missed because I never had it. But I'm happy you're here," I said.

She lay behind me and kissed between my shoulder blades. I kept expecting someone to barge into the room. The cleaner had noticed our entrance together. But why did I think she would make note of Emily's departure time? We could have been sisters, for all she knew. I hadn't seen something that looked specifically like judgement on her face, but maybe I still found my own paranoia written there. She had always been an affable type and made a point of saying hello to me in the hallway. I didn't know what I was so afraid of. I almost expected to incite the wrath of God. He might have struck me down the second everything advanced with Emily. But I was still intact, and then we made love and nothing disastrous occurred. It felt normal even though the sensations were all new to me. It was like she was part of my own body and had always been there. We lay hand in hand for a long time, staring at the ceiling and finding our own daydreams there.

We got dressed. I was glad we did because shortly after, there was a knock on the door. It was the girl that lived in the next room.

"We aren't allowed overnight guests," she said, in a surly tone.

I hadn't even noticed her on the way into my room. I wondered for a moment if she had a peephole. Ordinarily, she never seemed to leave her room.

"That's ok, Emily wasn't staying anyway," I said, apologetically.

When I shut the door, Emily looked at me with her arms crossed and a downward slant to her rosy mouth.

"What's wrong?" I asked. I realised in that second just how scared I was of upsetting her.

"You shouldn't have given in to that woman. Who is she?"

"A neighbour."

"She can't tell you what to do."

"She can tell the landlady."

"Don't be so afraid of what other people say and do."

"I can't get kicked out of here. Where would I go?"

"You could live with me."

She looked me dead centre in the eyes, so I knew she was serious. Maybe her boarding house had fewer rules, or maybe she was already thinking of where else we could live together. It was hard to know which. Emily didn't fear authority and I envied her that. I felt like I'd betrayed her in not defending her right to stay. We hadn't discussed her position in my life. It felt like we couldn't do that yet; not without it being inappropriate.

Emily put her coat on and gave me a forgiving kiss. "It's ok, don't worry about it."

She left, silently and I watched her leaving, her long coat sashaying behind her, like an apparition's gown. When she left, I was alone in the room with a bluebottle. It was buzzing against the window and kept bumping against it. It's stupidity and dirtiness disgusted me. I grabbed a day-old newspaper and swatted it with it, flicking its carcass out of the open window. I felt momentary guilt for being so ruthless with a form of life. But insect lives weren't worth anything in comparison to human lives. It was like feeling guilty for having to enlist an exterminator for a household infestation. It was just a fact of life. I just had a big heart underneath it all. I was sure no one else bothered to give it a second thought.

I didn't hear from Emily until I returned to work. She knew where I was, and she chose not to come to me. That said a lot. I stayed in my bedroom, feeling sorry for how I'd treated her. I remembered the pain on her face when I'd said she wouldn't be staying. I knew then that she'd expected she would be. I could call her a colleague or a friend, but she was much more than that. It wasn't the time to admit it though. I had never heard of women being publicly romantic or sexually involved. We might have been trailblazers in the community, but I wasn't comfortable advertising it. I didn't think Emily thought anything of it. But she could have been hunted down like in a witch trial and she would have scoffed at her captors. She was too clever for that kind of misconduct. Her quiet confidence in herself probably made most of her adversaries question themselves too. That was something I loved about her. I admitted it to myself. She had a comfortable ease with herself. We all know ourselves well, or think we do, but Emily seemed to have embraced herself in her entirety – the ugly as much as the good. And she was proud of it all. I wanted to hold her close to me and smell the scent of her hair. It always smelled clean – like unscented soap, which I was sure always had its own distinctive scent. It lingered in the room, and I wasn't sure if it remained behind after her visit or if my memory was just playing tricks on my senses.

I was nervous about going to work. I didn't know what I would find there. If Emily and I happened to be alone together all day, I didn't know how she might treat me. I might have felt like I knew her, but that didn't mean I knew what every one of her responses would be. She had an air of mystery about her that never lifted.

When I got to work, Emily had already opened up. I went in and sat down at my sewing machine, making a point to start threading the bobbin right away. I didn't know where else to look. Emily was sitting at her work desk, and I could feel her eyes boring into my forehead. I tried to casually lift my eyes to meet hers, but I knew it looked contrived. She was in the process of repairing a tear, but she paused mid-stitch. She examined me with her big open eyes. They were like vast lakes – the murky green kind that don't let you see through their surface. I realised when I looked into them, just how much I wanted to know her and how strong my feelings were for her. It wasn't something unimportant to me. It had the potential to bring about my emotional undoing.

"Are you angry with me?" I asked.

It was barely audible, but Emily shook her head straight away. It was like she could hear the words forming in my mind before they exited my mouth.

"No, I just thought you didn't want to be associated with me."

"I don't know how people would take it. I've never been in this situation before."

"I have. No one ever cottons on to what's truly happening. She probably thought we were a couple of friends having a sleepover."

"I'm still not allowed guests."

"If you want this to work, you're going to have to loosen up about things."

"Maybe I could come to your place instead?" I asked.

She nodded agreeably and returned to aligning the needle. That was the moment at which Ann barged in. She looked flustered and she was carrying a huge stack of laundry.

"My aunt got me to pick this up this morning – she needs me to wash them for her. Does she think I have nothing else to fill my time?"

We both looked at her, inexpressively.

"I can take your workload."

"We'll share it," I said, looking at Emily. She brightened up a lot.

That day was a trying one. We seemed to get a lot of new, difficult customers that didn't know the system and wanted to make it work to their advantage. Ann had an argument with one customer and decades later, she could have banned him for his borderline abusive behaviour, but in that day and age, women did what men told them to do. So, she gave him a great discount that he didn't deserve. It always seemed to be the types of men that were well dressed and obviously had disposable income that nit-picked over the trivial things. Thinking about that made me feel less sympathetic towards men as a species. It was hard to connect with them at times. The important people in my day-to-day life were women and they treated me fairly. Men seemed inconsistent.

Emily, and I kept each other's morale up. It was a day that tested us in every way, but we still made it through to the evening and got our day's pay. That was what was most important then – getting through the working day and still having a job to come back to the following one. I knew I was lucky in many ways. I was employed with people I liked to work with. Unemployment rates were soaring then, and everyone was striving to find whatever work they could. It could be competitive and cutthroat and those that knew the right people were in a better position to feed their families. I was relieved not to have one. I'd never felt the pressing need to bear children. It didn't appeal to me. It didn't seem like a tranquil mode of living, and I didn't want to have anyone dependent on me. I wasn't sure I could deliver the goods. I had made the decision I felt was the least selfish – pursuing my own goals and desires instead. I was still uncovering what those were each day.

There were many things I definitively knew about myself. For example, I was named after my mum's favourite aunt, I loved to work with my hands, and I was dexterous. I did what I could to avoid confrontation and I didn't like loud, unexpected noises. I could be jumpy, and I overthought everything until I didn't know how to put it into words. I loved potato bread and an Ulster fry. I couldn't stand cabbage and my least favourite meal as a child had been bubble and squeak. I was impatient when I was waiting for public transport and I always wanted to be in the city, connected to things, even if I had to live with factory fumes and little personal space. But I hadn't known about my sexual orientation, and my beliefs and values hadn't settled down into something fixed yet. I didn't know what I planned to do beyond the immediate future, but that didn't trouble me too much. I had a strong foundation upon which my life was constructed. My parents had ensured that, and I knew they would never see me struggling and fail to reach out a hand to help.

Where was I with my story? Sometimes I lose my train of thought because everything significant that happened has been overshadowed by what came later. I kept working away as a seamstress. It could have been tedious to some, but I didn't find it so. I found it satisfying because there was variety in what I was working on. I always imagined that Emily wanted more for herself. Belfast felt like a small place for her too – then. It was restrictive, with limited opportunities. We were doing better than most people living there. Still, I was always waiting for her to announce that she was leaving. But maybe, I believed our love would make her stay.

Chapter Four

I mightn't have gone to church like I should, but I tried to do the right thing. If I saw someone starving, I would happily have handed them food. If I saw some type of injustice, I'd stand up for what I thought was fair. It mightn't have meant much in the grand scheme of things, but I tried to be kind. I knew I'd still probably end up in hell when I died. With all I'd learnt as a kid, it was hard to switch off that engrained way of thinking. I'd been programmed to believe it since day one. Church sermons played in my back brain like songs I couldn't switch off. If I was honest with myself, I didn't believe as strongly in religion as I once had. It seemed harsh to me, and it didn't feel like a gentle way to live. I didn't necessarily call myself a lesbian because those feelings were all directed at one person. But I knew the teachings on such things. I would probably find eternal fire at my feet whenever I stepped off the earth, if I didn't repent. I didn't want to repent. A lifetime on Earth is a long time to be miserable. I couldn't think of many people in Northern Ireland that weren't, and most of them made religion the centre of their days and nights.

One day, I realised just how easy everything had been for me. I was in work and my job status, and everything else, changed in minutes. We were working through our usual workload, thinking our own quiet thoughts when fire tore through the place. It started with an iron on a dress, and it ended in permanent closure. Not everyone had insurance then. It was more of a luxury for the elite than an everyday expense. That was the end of my career in the shop. I had the money to pay that week's rent, and that was all I had. But that wasn't the main thing that bothered me; it was the state in which it left Ann. Her life was contained in that small shop, and she looked like she'd lost a child when she looked over the charred remains. We knew we had been lucky to be there, but you can never see that with complete clarity until something is gone. Emily didn't seem shaken by the experience. Maybe she saw it as her pass to freedom – an excuse to get out of the spot she was stuck in. I never heard from her again after that day. She waited until the fire brigade extinguished the flames, and then she quietly slipped out. I thought she'd call by to see me later that night, but she didn't. I waited for a long time. The deathly silence made me feel sick. I was facing the prospect of having to return to my family home and start from scratch, but all I could think about was Emily. I waited for her for two days straight, bathing in my own tears. The bedsheets were saturated, but I couldn't move my face from that spot. I was so numb I could barely feel it. I don't know why I expected the affair to have a happier ending, especially at that time. No one was going to praise our strange union – not then – nor decades later.

I found a new start that week. Ann wasn't as lucky. I heard she returned to her hometown. I started working in another place washing clothes, but it was harder work. I didn't get to sew anymore, my hands were scrubbed raw, and the pay was less. I could still pay for my room, so it didn't much matter, but life felt empty without Emily. I realised how much time I'd been spending with her - or thinking about her when she wasn't there. I had to banish those thoughts from my mind because I knew she wasn't coming back. She had probably moved on to something exciting. I wasn't exciting; I was straightforward and easily satisfied. I still needed more though. Work, room, work, room was not a good pattern to have. I got little social interaction. My boss wasn't the type of person you could have a good time with. She was stern and had strict boundaries between employer and employee, and I knew she saw me as less important than herself.

I decided to help out at a local soup kitchen in my free time. I had passed it on my walk every day. I needed to be reminded that there was always someone more miserable than me. I might have lost Emily, but I wasn't without a job, family or home. The food they served to the people was like gruel. It was something I'd only thought existed in Dickensian fiction. I felt sad offering that to the people that visited, and they were so grateful to get it. I was surprised by how many visited it daily. I'd been vaguely aware of it being open before that, but I hadn't realised how essential it was to the community. It was obviously a lifeline to many people. I felt honoured to be given an apron. It made my sadness wane, working there. It felt like I was contributing to something bigger than myself. Those were the times I felt happiest in the world: when I didn't have time to consider my own troubles.

I got to know some of the regulars. There was a family that came in every day, and I loved seeing the kids. They were always upbeat despite the circumstances they had just come from. I knew theirs must have been bad. The parents were both unemployed and they had nowhere to stay. But the kids were still playful, and they gave us the brightest grins when they came inside. They enjoyed running around the shined floors of the big hall, hearing their voices echoing. After they'd run off some energy, they came to get something to eat. I always tried to save some extra for them. On days when we had crusty bread, I put some aside for them out of sight. I thought they needed it most. Maybe it was wrong of me to decide that, but children in need always seemed worse off to me than adults in the same position. It was like they were being robbed of a worry-free childhood. Maybe at that time, it was common to live like that, but I knew what it was like to have a real childhood and it killed me, seeing their deprivation.

That was how I filled my evenings. I didn't spend much time in my room, other than for sleeping. I went to public baths on my nights off so I could wash and stay fresh. There weren't any bathrooms in the boarding house – just a toilet and basin. I made the best of myself that I could at the sink. That was what everyone did then. It didn't feel problematic; we didn't know any different. When I think of the ease with which people can attend to their basic needs nowadays, sometimes I feel sorry for them. They don't have to be resourceful or creative, and it's harder to feel grateful when everything comes to you too easily. For the duration of my life, I had to improvise with what I had. That was never a bad thing. Sometimes, I get to watch moments of modern living through a window onto the world – when I'm rewarded for good behaviour.

When I was working at washing clothes, my hands were always tired. I couldn't even bear to soak them when I got home. They had been wet all day and were wrinkled from too much soap and water. It was just the way things were then. People didn't complain about things. They were happy to be tired, because it usually meant they were getting paid, or they had somewhere to stay.

I stayed there for a few years. I never met another romantic partner in that time, nor did I feel the need to. I didn't feel like anything was missing. It just wasn't something that I naturally needed to survive. I didn't feel the need to advance further within the working world, so long as I could cover my basic needs. I didn't aspire to own a house. It was practically unheard of for a single woman to do that then. The bank probably would have refused to give me the loan, so I didn't even consider asking for one.

There was a man whose clothing we washed that came to pick them up each week. I knew he liked me because he'd always try to linger and draw out the conversation. I was pleasant but I was quiet too. I didn't want to encourage him too much. He probably had grand designs in his mind of the kind of couple we could become, but I knew it was impossible. He was wasting his breath on wooing me. It had no effect on my heart. It just irritated me, like a pet that follows you everywhere you go, never giving you a chance to miss it. I knew he wasn't unattractive – objectively-speaking – but he wasn't attractive to me. My boss seemed to like him. I thought she'd like to see me married off because she probably wanted rid of me. I could never do anything right in her eyes. But maybe she would have been the same way with any other employee in the world. She was just the type that feels better when she's making someone else feel inferior. She was a perfectionist and she never let a mistake slide by unnoticed. Her company was difficult to endure, but I was so busy I couldn't dwell on it too much. My special visitor got annoying after a while, but he was relentless in his pursuit of me. He wasn't going to stop coming. He had me cornered in my place of work, and the worst thing was – he was so nice about it. If he had been obnoxious and pushy, it would have been easier to resist his advances. He kept offering me the promise of a better life, but I didn't want it.

Then, my mum got sick. She was always one of those hardy people that never caught a cold. But when she did get sick, she really was ill. She had cancer and they didn't have as many options for treatment then. Her own mother had had it, and the disease had killed her. I was so worried about her. If you had money, you could get better treatment, so I finally agreed to marry Fred: the man that visited our shop with such constancy. He had asked me multiple times, even though we'd had only limited interactions.

People were quick to commit to something then. He didn't know who I really was. Maybe it was better that way. Maybe that's what has gone wrong since. Divorce is popular, but so is delving into your problems and sharing every single one of them with your partner. Do you or they really need to know it all? That is something I wonder in the few moments of stillness I have to think. I mull over periods of my life and things that should or could have been different. I get moments of peace in which to consider that, but overall, I'm too busy to be able to give it much attention.

I knew that in a way, I was using Fred. He was a kindly soul. I told myself he had asked for it, by being so determined to win me over. Maybe he didn't even care if I didn't love him. He just wanted to have me, like a medal to flash to his friends. That made me feel like what I was doing wasn't utterly selfish. I needed his money, but I didn't want it for purely selfish purposes. Material things meant nothing to me but getting the best treatment my mum could get did matter. I owed her a lot and I wanted her to make it to a good age.

I was reluctant to give up my little room. I suggested keeping it, for when I was working, but Fred couldn't understand that. He said I had no need to work, and in a way, I was glad to give up the hard labours that wore the skin from my hands. My hands were never dainty or delicate; they were always dry and flaky and covered in sores. I didn't know why it didn't put him off me, but he seemed to have a fascination with me that I would never understand. It didn't seem to wane, and that was probably lucky for my family. I had never told them about Emily. I still thought that no one would understand that inclination of mine.

I left behind my little room and the flies that plagued me dancing around in the window. I didn't think there would be any in Fred's house. It was more of an estate than a house. I didn't want to just become a useless appendage of his. The soup kitchen was still there, waiting for someone to fill my post. I sacrificed a lot in marrying him – not just my independence, but my romantic possibilities and my sense of purpose. I thought that was a fair exchange in a way. He was getting me, and I was getting his financial aid.

It was all going to be OK – I told myself it was. I'd never felt so mournful when I'd entered a new place before. That room that didn't belong to me was my first independent home. It mightn't have been pretty to look at; it was dark, and the décor was tired, but it had a feel to it, like it had slowly been suffused with the experiences I'd had there. That made it beautiful and important to me. It had always been inevitable that I would leave but it hurt, thinking of someone else staying there. In my mind, it would always be mine. I pulled the drapes as I said my goodbyes to it. My entire life could be packed up into a single suitcase. Once it was, all personal marks of mine were effaced. I paid my last week's rent to the landlady. She didn't ask where I was going to or why. So long as she was getting timely payments, that was all that mattered. I was nameless and faceless to her.

Our wedding ceremony was stark in its simplicity. There was nothing particularly romantic about it. I wore the virginal white dress, and I had the freshly picked roses. I carried them with a certain pride and dignity, knowing why I was going through with it. It was self-sacrifice. Fred looked flushed. I couldn't tell if he was genuinely moved by the occasion or if he'd had a drink, or several, for his nerves. Overall, he was relaxed, and I was uptight. I could feel every fibre of my being fighting against it, but I kept walking forwards anyway.

The service felt to me more like a funeral than a wedding. Not many people were there. My parents attended, but Fred's side of the church was eerily quiet. Maybe that didn't bode well, I thought. People that didn't have a connection with family or friends were usually lacking something. There was no celebratory feel to the place. The white stone of the building made it as chilled as my heart felt in my own chest.

I said empty words to my groom – reciting them after the pastor and trying to enliven them with a kind of melody, but they were as dull as dead love. I felt for Fred though. I could feel the power behind his words – he meant them on the deepest level. I just couldn't generate the same feelings. He was strange looking – like something from a Mary Shelley novel. I was sure my parents questioned my reasons for going through with the ceremony. But when I looked at my mother's face, so white with illness, that was the only confirmation I needed that I was doing the right thing. It wasn't about me – it was a day that so much more hinged upon.

Chapter Five

I was unhappier than I'd ever been upon my arrival in the boarding house. I could still remember that day with crystal clarity. I'd come from a warm family home, and I'd never lived anywhere else. I couldn't fathom what it would be to live elsewhere. I didn't know what to expect, and what awaited me was less than hospitable. Without the decoration of my belongings, when I arrived, it was like stepping into an uninhabitable tunnel. The room was long and funnelled from the hallway towards the bed. That was the only part of the room that had any space in it. There were simple pieces of furniture – a bed, a bedside table, a wardrobe. There were no lamps, no personal features, no personality at all. It was funny when I recalled that first moment, just how much I had warmed to the place. It was like a fond friend I kept in my heart – one I could never see again due to circumstances getting in the way, but one that would always remain clear and crisp there – like an untouched photograph.

My new place of residence was opulent, but that didn't make it homely to me. Fred was a bachelor. He'd been alone for so long that you couldn't take his bachelorhood out of him. He lived quietly. There was no homely noise about the place. Maybe it was just so vast and hollow that it wasn't possible for it to do anything other than echo our lonely footsteps. I hated the sound of my own steps on the tiled floors. Everything was ornate, but I couldn't stand the sight of it. Fred was kind to me, but he quickly picked up on my lack of desire for him. We fell into a friendly mode of interaction. He was a companion I met with for mealtimes and in the evenings, but we parted company before bed. I remembered the look of hurt on his face when I'd first flinched at his touch. He was a sensitive soul, even if he was determined to get what he wanted. He never pushed that with me, and I appreciated it.

We had one conversation about having children and I quickly shut the subject down. He knew not to broach it again. I told him I wasn't maternal – I'd had certain experiences that had indicated to me that I wouldn't make a good mother. Fred resigned himself to that. He probably felt lucky I was there at all. His house was more like a country estate, and it was a solitary place to stay. He sacrificed companionship for the sake of beauty and peacefulness. He seemed to think that was a fair exchange.

Fred was always kind to my parents. He didn't see his own very often. He said they were different to him and that they avoided each other unless events necessitated a connection with them. They were related, but they weren't insofar as how they viewed the world. Fred confided in me. He told me he felt like he'd been transposed there and that he had never belonged. He treated my parents like they were his surrogate ones. That only increased my feelings of guilt in how I had treated him.

I did have a conscience. I had always had an overactive one. But I suppressed it to get by; to serve one moral need before another. My mum's health was ailing more and more each day and Fred was prepared to fund her treatment. There was little that could be done for her, but her chances of recovery were improved by money. I guess not much has changed in the course of time in that respect.

I knew I spent far too much time in my bedroom. There was a large amount of land around us, but I didn't make use of it. It was unseemly then for women to wander on their own, at least, it was where I was living. Fred didn't have any close friends nearby, but he cared about what the community thought. They were a judgemental crowd. I only had the displeasure of making their acquaintance when they landed on our doorstep, inviting themselves in for a cup of tea. It was a world I didn't belong to. I was born to work – not for idle entertainment. My parents rarely visited us, even though they were benefiting from our union. They liked Fred but I never felt like they thought he was the right person for me. They knew me better than I'd even realised they did. Sometimes when my mother would go to discuss the subject with me, she'd stumble on her words and then stop. I could see the whirr of her mental process as it took place behind her eyes. Whatever she had to say could be left unsaid and I'd still know what it was. The doctor she was seeing was a famous physician in London, and everyone had been delighted when he'd moved into the community. He was the closest thing we had to a foreign arrival then, and it brought a bit of excitement to the place.

I always found him a bit stuck up. Maybe his way of speaking was just so upper class it made me feel uncouth next to him. I was self-conscious of my "r's" and my more pronounced wording of things. We didn't spend a great deal of time in each other's company, but I still had to interact with him intermittently, and when I did, I always felt like a second-class citizen. That fact made me hopeful he had some sort of divine power when it came to healing his patients – because he thought he was above us. My mother was the sickest I'd ever seen anyone. It was frightening to watch the development of her illness, but I still believed that she would make it through and that she'd be declared well again. She had a strong constitution, so she had to recover. My father was dependent on her too. He was always lingering beside her, and he looked lost when she went into another room. I feared what would happen to him in her absence. But I didn't worry too often about it because I trusted the skill of the doctor we had at our service.

Fred didn't resent the cost. He would have given me every penny of his money if it meant that he could keep me there, looking out the window at the world passing us by. It felt like everyone else was living outside the house, even if their existence was harder than ours. I thought of my old room and longed to go back there, but there was no chance I ever could. It was probably inhabited by another directionless young woman by then – someone tiding themselves over on the lowest available wage. It was sad in a way, that I envied those penniless workers. I felt like I'd lost an important part of myself.

If my mum got better, I vowed to leave the place, even if I had to run against my own morals to do it. Quietly remaining there would be like giving up on life for good. I wasn't the type to lie down and take whatever was doled out, so I knew it was something finite. I felt ill with guilt but pretending to be someone I wasn't could only continue for so long.

I'd taken an early retirement, of sorts. There was no housework to keep myself busy with. We had maids that completed the daily tasks. My job was to sit and look pretty – another ornament in an already over-decorated room. There was fine bone china everywhere, and floral arrangements. Everything was pale and insipid. I almost preferred things to be depressingly dark, like in the boarding house. At least they weren't posing as something more perfect than they truly were. Dingy rooms with age marks were preferable any day to me.

I sat in a regal looking chair that made my back ache. It felt like I was aging every single day. I was bored and boredom was feeding into sadness. Checking on my mother was the only diversion I had. I went to their home every week and made sure she was comfortable and had everything she needed. Fred had paid for help for their household too, so I didn't get to do much more than fluff her pillows and wipe her clammy brow. She closed her eyes over when I did it, like a sleep-ready baby. I didn't like seeing her in a position of weakness; it didn't suit her at all. Some people are better designed for periods of prolonged sickness. They're happy to rest in bed all day, to receive fruit baskets and greetings cards and to play the patient. My mother didn't appreciate those things. She wanted to be on her feet, always active and ready to help someone else. I knew she found it degrading, finding herself in that position, and it was sad to watch.

I tried my best to show kindness to Fred. I ate with him dutifully at each mealtime. We talked about my mum and about the weather and about anything else unrelated to us that we could think of. It was like having a distant neighbour between meals. We occupied different parts of the house. Sometimes I thought he wasn't suited to marriage either. Maybe that was what he had liked about me – he'd sensed that I wouldn't expect much of him as a husband. I knew he was mostly with me for my looks. He'd made that adequately clear. He was always studying my physical attributes, but he didn't seem to want to get to know what lay at the depths of my soul. I didn't think his own reached too far down. If a person of depth was a well, he was just a dip in the ground that periodically collected water.

The house we lived in always made me feel strange. It was too cold to be liveable; like it was designed for a cold-blooded creature. The rooms were dim. No hint of sunlight ever got in. It was clean enough that if the sun had penetrated it, not one flyaway hair would have shown up in the sunlight. We never had the chance for that, and I ached for a little human detail in the place. It was like no one lived there. It was just like a stage set – held up for the duration of the show, waiting to be dismantled immediately afterwards. The vaulted ceilings were grand and gave an antique feel to everything, but they were impractical and didn't encourage heat to grow either. It would have made a model museum. I could imagine visitors being in awe of aspects of it, but it was different when you lived there. I never felt like I was completely alone there – and not in a positive way. It was like there was something belonging to another dimension lurking there, waiting for me – for its moment to strike. I'd never been more uncomfortable in any other place in my life and by then, I was well into my twenties.

I still thought about Emily. I have been lying if I said I didn't. She was still the most significant person in my life, and it drove me mad not knowing what had become of her. I knew she wouldn't be thinking about me at the same moment, or any moment thereafter. She was a person without attachments. It hurt to admit that to myself, but it was true. I knew it was pointless giving any of my thoughts to her. She was gone for good, and I had subscribed to a different life. I knew I'd have to leave that situation behind me without ever knowing what had become of it.

Fred paid for everything. It made me feel useless, but my mum seemed to be brightening up. Her face was less pale than it had been. I was less concerned about her. But those are usually the times when the unpredictable happens. I relaxed too much in that respect. She suddenly deteriorated. She was hospitalised and then moved into a hospice within weeks. I could read about the strain of it on my father's face. He wanted to go with her. He would have happily slept on the hard floor if it meant he got to be close to her. I told him to stay with us, and he accepted, but he spent all his time at the hospital, falling asleep in the visitor's chair.

I couldn't bear to look at Mum. She was in a terrible state. She was weeping. I'd never known her to do that – not at inconsequential things, or even at the things that merited it. She was stoic, like most of the women from her generation. They'd lived through wars and horrors of their own that they'd likely never speak about. It carried a kind of honour with it – keeping secrets that had never been asked to be kept. I sat on the edge of the bed, reading bits of books to her – her literature had always been an integral part of her life. She'd read constantly for as long as I could remember. She had more books than some public libraries had – at least, she did in the volume of good quality novels. She seemed contented when I read to her – as much as she could be, staying there.

But overall, she was rapidly worsening. She had lost her hair and she wore a scarf wrapped around her head. My mum's hair had been a matter of pride. She had always got it dyed and had sets done. She looked like a different person without it. I thought she had a stark kind of beauty in its absence, but I never told her that. I didn't want to hurt her.

Fred waited with me whenever he wasn't otherwise engaged. He worked long hours as a bank executive, often going away for work. He was needed in the city a lot and I always felt a huge wave of relief when he went to stay in a hotel. I knew it was wrong to feel that way. He had opened his heart and his home to me – offering it to me as my own, and he didn't invade my space. He let me stay in my quarters and he stayed in his. Maybe you just get easily irritated when you're somewhere you don't want to be. When he sat next to me at my mother's bedside, all I could hear was his heavy breathing. Maybe it was that way because he was so stressed, but my tolerance for it was too low. I felt like I was becoming a bad person, if I hadn't already stumbled into that territory with my decision to marry him. I didn't know what he could possibly derive from our union. It didn't serve him in any way. I wanted to work again, to put money into the pot, but Fred didn't want that. When I quietly suggested returning to my work, he told me I was a married woman – not one of the bottom classes. But that was where I was more comfortable. When we travelled to the hospital, we went in a private car. There was a driver we paid to transport us everywhere. On our way there, we'd often pass through the city, and I'd see glimpses of the old life I'd had. There were women in worn, grey and brown dresses. They were occupied with their children and with carrying large loads of laundry and food. It was back-breaking work, but I envied them. They were living the high life, as far as I was concerned. They had the freedom to do things considered demeaning to women in the upper classes. I wanted to get my hands dirty too.

My mother passed away in her sleep at the hospice. They phoned the house to let us know. I didn't pick up first, so Fred knew about my mother before I did. That fact upset me a lot. I still had a deep connection with my parents, and I wanted to be their port in a savage storm. We were invited to see my mother's body. I didn't know how I felt about that, but I went anyway. I was afraid to say no in case I changed my mind about it later, and it was too late to act. When we walked into the little parlour at the funeral home, her casket was open. Her body looked miniscule lying there. Maybe it was just seeing her boxed up that gave that impression. She looked short and compact, and fragile. When I looked into her face, her eyes were closed, and she didn't look like herself at all – even when she was sleeping. It was a strange sensation, looking at the person that had brought me into the world in the face and barely recognising them. I knew she was already long gone. She was far from her body, perhaps watching us from a great height. I started to sob, and Fred took me in his firm grasp. I didn't want him to touch me, and I grew limp while he held me. My father spent time with my mother separately. He stayed there for hours on end, and we were called to collect him when the home was closing for the evening. He looked haunted when he came out to the car. He sat in the backseat without saying a word, watching our view of the world go by the window, his eyes following each bit until it was gone.

Chapter Six

A week after my mother died, my father passed away too. It felt like too much to endure, losing both parents at once. We had been a unit and no one else meant as much to me as they did. It made sense that they both accompanied each other to whatever the next stage was. I hoped the Christian teachings I'd been taught were right then. They hadn't felt relevant to my life until death came into the equation. It was easy to brush something aside until later when it felt like it wasn't looming. I was confronted with my own mortality then too, and the thought that I might die in miserable circumstances. Something had to be done about it. I thought about Fred too. He deserved greater happiness than I was able to give him. I wondered if a divorced man of his age would find it in himself to look for another love. I suspected it might be too late for him. I felt like I had ruined his life in so many ways. I owed him something, but nothing I could think of would ever repay him if I initiated a separation.

The funerals of my parents didn't feel real. I was so much in shock I felt disengaged from the entire thing. Maybe that was for the best. Fred tried to relate to me in recounting stories of his disappointment in his own parents, but they were still living, and his fables only served to irritate me. I sat next to a distant cousin in the church at the first service, and a family friend filled the seat next to me at another. I knew if anyone noticed we were sitting apart, they would think it looked weird, but I was allowed to do as I felt necessary at my own parents' funerals. There were so many flowers in the room it gave it a sickly scent. It was like the odour of decaying fruit pervaded the room. Everyone else seemed to be immune to the cloying scent. Once the burials were over, it felt like it was truly over. It had been easier in a way, waiting for the funerals. It still felt like there was something more to do for them. After their deaths, they were buried side by side in a plot. That gave me some solace – thinking that they'd rest forever next to each other. But it felt like the purpose of my marriage had passed. Time and money had been spent, but really, it hadn't helped in the end. I knew I'd made a mistake in getting married for the reasons I did. I felt like I owed Fred a lifetime of debt too. He'd put himself out so much to get my mother the best available treatment and it hadn't succeeded. It felt like he'd wasted himself on me too.

I quickly withdrew when we went home. Fred hardly noticed. We hadn't been inseparable to begin with. I think once the funerals were over, he viewed them as a type of closure – like there was no need to talk about them anymore. There was nothing more to be done. He'd ask me intermittently if I was ok, but it felt like more of a general question than one specific to that situation. He'd been fond of my parents, but I didn't get the sense that Fred got overly attached to anyone. He just thought he was to me. Had he been asked if he could survive without me, I knew his answer would be a definite "no," but I didn't see what I did for him, beyond standing there like a statue at times.

Sitting in my bedroom was driving me to madness. I felt like I might as well have been locked in a tower. The windows overlooked the huge gardens, but they didn't cheer my heart one bit. It looked like everything had wilted with the change of season. It was time for nature to sleep, along with my hopes. I couldn't see an exit route and I couldn't see the possibility of a future moment where things were improved. I slept in my four-poster bed, the sheets so cold against my skin that I shivered. No matter how long I lay there for, the coldness didn't seem to subside. I had one of those heavy, old-fashioned hot water bottles – the metal kind. It was placed in my bed to heat it before I went to sleep, but I'd been retiring so early, the maids hadn't bothered delivering it. It must have been obvious that I didn't want anyone's company - not even a knock at the door and the offer of luxury. I knew I should have been happy; that was what made me unhappiest. I was supposed to be thriving in the lap of luxury, but I couldn't stand it. I couldn't bear the ease of being rich – there was nothing to preoccupy me or to distract my thoughts from the darkness they always found.

I lay, unblinking, staring at the wall. There were shadows on it, made by the furnishings. I could hear the wind making the trees swish outside. It was a wild night, and I wished I could appreciate the cosiness of where I was snuggled up. But I couldn't. I had to find a way out of my dull nightmare. It was like I was trapped in a recurring dream – one where very little happened. That was almost worse than one with shocking events; at least those would have created a diversion for me. I knew I had to get out quickly, even though shame would inevitably follow. I'd ruin whatever reputation I had, and I knew I'd have to move away and start afresh. I still didn't know how to break it to Fred in a way he would accept. No matter how many ways I worded it in my mind, it never sounded acceptable. So, I'd end up staring out at the pallid landscape instead. It always looked misted from behind the glass of my room. There was nothing keeping me prisoner there, besides my own inertia. Fred had always encouraged me to go outside, and I knew he wouldn't stop me wandering free if I chose to do so. It was Spring and birds were awakening in nature again. You could hear their faithful singing – a salutation to a better season. It gave me the urge to take flight too.

I broke the news to Fred the next morning at breakfast time. He was sitting at the far end of the table, making sterile conversation between flipping the pages of his newspaper. He didn't look like he was really taking it in; he looked like he was just looking for somewhere to hide from me. I couldn't find the appetite for my breakfast. It was just tea and dry toast. The butter had settled into the bread long before my arrival, but it made no difference to the taste. It was like chewing on sandpaper. My mouth was already dry, but that always happened when I was anxious about saying something. There were no words that would make it OK. I just had to dive into the conversation I knew I'd regret having in many future private moments.

"I've decided I can't continue to live here," I said.

I knew I sounded detached and business-like. But isn't marriage business-like when you think about the basics of it? Mine had been in every way, from my side of the bed, table and house. There was a pot of coffee on the table, sitting untouched, eggs, a variety of cold drinks. We were spoiled and I was miserable. It was strange how so many poor people thought money would be the magical corrector pen applied to their existence. It would make everything that had previously been wrong tolerable, if not right. It was like funnelling whiskey down the neck of a bad day.

I pushed my plate aside – not in a rude way; just in a final way – like bringing your cutlery to meet in the middle of your plate when you've finished a meal. Fred was no longer touching his food either. He still hadn't said anything, and the silence was sitting before me like it was demanding I fill it.

"I'm sorry," I said, "I really am."

Fred shook his head. "If you were sorry, you wouldn't have brought it up."

"I can't suppress my own sadness just to keep yours at bay. Are you really happy with the way things are?"

"No, but I'm happier than I would be if you left. I can't live in an empty house again."

"It wouldn't be empty."

"Staff isn't the same thing as family."

"You've known most of them longer than you've known me."

"They don't show me any affection."

"Do I?" I asked, and I could see that inside his mind he was being honest with himself about the disappointment I'd brought into his life.

He shrugged his shoulders and pushed his chair back from the table, getting to his feet.

"Do what you want – I can't stop you."

I gave him a weary smile – at least I thought I did.

He smiled sadly at me, and I knew he understood me, even if he didn't like it.

Chapter Seven

The next day, I left. I packed my suitcase – only bringing the items I'd had when I'd arrived. I didn't want to take anything else from Fred. I felt terrible enough as it was. He'd been kindly, even as I'd left him. He didn't come to say goodbye when I was climbing into the car, but he had arranged to have it pick me up. He didn't know where I was going to after that, and I supposed he wouldn't have wanted me to tell him. I didn't look back as I drove away from the house. I didn't have the desire to see the final frame before I left. It made me sad that I was hurting Fred, but other than that, I felt nothing but relief. It was like I was a caged animal released after a long stint in a cage three sizes too small.

The driver was taciturn, and he didn't even look at me in the rear-view mirror. I familiarised myself with his eyes while he drove, but he didn't once meet mine. I wondered how well he knew Fred. Maybe he felt like he was betraying him in transporting me away from the house. I wondered if Fred had told the staff that I'd left yet. I didn't suppose any of them would feel any particular sadness about it. I had been like an extra chair there – something everyone could see and that got in people's way but that didn't inspire any affection in them and that there was no use for ninety-nine percent of the time. I knew I wouldn't have been sad to see myself go, had I not been stuck in my own body, forced to accompany myself wherever my rebellious will took me.

The scenery wasn't beautiful, even though I knew it was on an aesthetic level. It was misty and morose; like an indicator that nothing hopeful was to come. But I knew that what had happened had just infected the day with its sombreness. I didn't know what I would do beyond that day. Fred had given me a small sum of money for a place to stay. I found the cheapest one I could in town. It felt good to be back in the dirty city streets again. I felt more like myself there. Maybe I was made to live in the heart of the metropolis, cleaning dirt for a living. Once you've been a washerwoman once, it's hard to let go of that part of yourself. You get used to having wrinkled hands that never rest. Stopping and sitting still feel foreign to you – unhealthy even. I knew that I should have gone with my initial impression of Fred. He had made my skin move in ripples across my bones. Sometimes someone just has a smell that repels you, or something unqualifiable about them. It's probably genetics at work – trying to protect you from a bad match. That was what I thought later, when I educated myself more and knew the details of those things. That day, I just thought I should have listened to my gut feeling sooner.

My mother had never seemed delighted to know Fred, despite the fact he had offered her so much support. The whole scenario hadn't been fair to him, and I felt terrible about it. Sometimes when you act for your own self-preservation, people assume that you're selfish. But really, you're just reacting instinctively to something you know isn't safe for you – isn't safe for the state of your soul. I wished I could repay him all the money I'd taken. I'd viewed it as payment for my services – like he was buying a bride. He seemed happy with his side of the deal, but I never could be with mine. I knew that Fred must have known I never loved him. I didn't think that I was even capable of loving a man. When I thought of his physicality, it repulsed me. His body was so straight and toned. There were no waves in it and nothing soft about it that felt humanly warming to me. The few times I had allowed Fred to enter my bed, I'd quivered at his touch, and he hadn't forced me to go any further. I just wanted him to be Emily. I could never shake her from my mind. Hers was an image I would have done anything to dislodge, but I didn't know how to. She'd been my initiation into the world of romance. That was important in itself. Fred couldn't outshine her. No man could. I never fantasised about women – just Emily. I felt like I was attracted more to her as a person than I was to her because she was female. I wondered if I even had the capacity to love or to desire someone again. I felt lonely without her, but it was lonelier being with someone that wasn't her.

When the car drew up at the area's cheapest boarding house, I was relieved to have arrived. It was the shabbiest building I'd ever seen, but it was still a place to sleep for a while. I was desperate to lie down. I had the kind of tiredness that only comes from sadness – like the kind that comes to you after a bereavement – when you could lie in bed day and night, never feeling any more rested. I knew that even if my mind wanted to keep me awake that evening, my body wouldn't allow it. That was one blessing that came with terrible upheaval – you got physically exhausted, and physical exhaustion defeated mental wakefulness every time.

I didn't bother saying a long goodbye to the driver. He'd done nothing to make the situation any less uncomfortable. Maybe that was by design. I still didn't know his exact connection to Fred. It could have been his brother, for all I knew. That highlighted to me just how little I knew of Fred, even after spending years together. I entered the building, my suitcase in my hand. It was light enough I didn't need help to carry it. I didn't have anything of any worth in my hands. My mother hadn't left much behind her. She didn't treasure possessions either. She'd left me a single necklace, that I wore around my neck. I never took it off to the point I forgot that it was even there. It meant more to me than anything else, but I realised I felt much better when I wasn't burdened by belongings.

The lady at the desk took my payment for a week and told me where I could find my room. The place badly needed swept and dusted. It was dingy, but I loved it. I instantly felt at home there. I wouldn't have traded it for anything more pleasing to the eyes. There was a homeliness to the disorder and the landlady's sourness was familiar to me. I preferred that to someone putting on airs for me. I was never meant to have a servant – I was meant to serve – but not a husband. I didn't know if I would ever get a divorce. I'd felt like it was too much to ask of Fred. No one I'd met had got a divorce at that time in Northern Ireland. It was too religious a place to approve of the undoing of such a Christly contract. I didn't believe there was anything wrong with it, but I also knew I'd never remarry, so it didn't matter to me if I remained married by law. I never had to accompany Fred anywhere again, or hold his hand, or pretend to be happy with him, and that was more important to me than any divorce paper. I went to unpack my few items in my bedroom. When I opened the door, I was greeted by its grubby familiarity. The bedsheets probably hadn't been laundered between guests, the floor hadn't been brushed, there was a strange odour that could probably be blamed on the number of previous occupants and the lack of cleaning, but I didn't mind.

None of that mattered to me. What mattered was having my freedom, even if its setting was far beneath ordinary. I came to learn that the girl living in the adjoining room was severely disturbed, but even that didn't scare me off. She had her troubles, but they only manifested in her calling out in different voices to herself. It sounded like she was having an animated conversation with a visitor, but she was the only one to ever set foot in that room. If I passed her in the hallway, I didn't have anything to do with her. She always looked disorientated and like she wouldn't be able to answer questions with any degree of honesty anyway. She was living in her own world, and so long as hers didn't disturb mine too much, it didn't matter.

I wondered if Fred had been driven to madness too. I knew he would struggle to resettle himself in the house without a wife. Our relationship might have always been a façade, but I knew Fred thought more of it than I had. I straightened up my room, folding the blankets and making a half-hearted attempt at unpacking. I didn't have anything that I had grown used to in the house: tea made for me, dinners served to our liking, laundry taken care of. Those days were gone and that didn't bother me at all. I was grateful to be standing where I was, even if I experienced small seconds of self-doubt. Doesn't everyone experience those? Some people are good at masking their feelings and speaking a kind of double talk all the time. But everyone must doubt their choices sometimes. You can't get it right every minute of your life.

I didn't hear from Fred after I moved to the boarding house. I'd half-expected to if I was truly honest with myself. He'd always been overeager and overprotective, but I didn't hear a word from him. I supposed that was testament to the severity of my treatment of him. I stayed put. It was a grotty household, but it was better than nothing and I couldn't afford to upgrade my living options. I took up a job washing dishes in the house. There was a constant stream of them. The kitchen fed all the occupants together. We were always eating something that was satisfying, but never tasty, out of a large casserole dish. I was glad of the warmth in my tummy. It was the only motherly comfort that I received since the death of my mother. Everyone helped themselves with a ladle when they came in from their respective jobs. We were all equally poorly paid, and we had a strange kind of allegiance to each other, considering the fact we came from opposing worlds.

I was washing dishes day and night — at least, it felt like I was. The lady that ran the house did some baking on the side. She made loaves of bread to sustain us throughout the cold nights. It was still deathly cold in the place at night. I don't think many in Northern Ireland had heating then, so we were nothing special in that respect. Sometimes it is in the least likely places that opportunity lands in your lap. I was just getting on with my work. It was tedious, but I was glad of it because it filled my days. I met a new lady that had moved into the house. She was beautiful in the classic way, but she hadn't taken care of herself. She probably didn't have the money to do it. None of us did. I had used up all of Fred's money on my accommodation and anything else I earned was immediately spent on sustaining my stay there. Daisy was the name of the new arrival and we instantly hit it off. She had the humour my life had been lacking for so long.

She was always playing practical jokes – putting surprises for me in the kitchen, to cheer me up, or to make me jump. She was playful in a way adults usually never were. It was normally beaten out of them by their responsibilities, but she had somehow evaded that. The landlady wasn't keen on her. I could see that every time she walked into the room. She was the first person since Emily I felt anything real for. I was worried about her wellbeing, and I didn't want her to get thrown out of the house.

"Just tone it down," I said to her, as I was clearing away the breakfast dishes. "You don't want to lose your room here."

"There's always another room in another house," she said, flippantly.

"I won't be living there."

"Well, we could still visit each other."

I knew when she said that that I cared more than she did. I needed to see her every day. I didn't need anything specific from her; I just needed to see her there. I didn't like sitting alone in my room anymore and I looked for any excuse to leave it. But sometimes, Daisy was busy in her own, or she went out and I didn't know what kind of a life she was leading. I felt jealous though – of imagined people that might captivate her. I didn't know if she visited any men. She didn't strike me as being interested in them. She'd never made a reference to any but living in the house we were in made everyone like that. We were living so separately from men that it was easy to forget their existence. Daisy had golden hair that fell around her face in a way that was too lovely to describe in mere words. She was always smiling and that was her charm. I wanted to get closer to her. We'd sit, head-to-head, like schoolgirls laughing, but it never became anything more than that. I realised I didn't love Emily anymore. I

41

couldn't have said that until that point. It was a relief not to pine for her anymore. It was emotionally exhausting doing that with no end in sight. I realised how sad I'd been and even though it felt like I deserved a certain sadness, it didn't make it any easier to endure.

I sat in my room, watching the flies headbutting the windowpane. There were earwigs that moved across the floor and some other unidentified beetle-like creatures. It was like an infestation, and I realised that I hadn't seen a bug in Fred's house. It was too clean for that; like they instinctively knew not to enter. I didn't notice that they hadn't been there until they were there constantly. The bugs that walked on the floor bothered me less than the ones that rattled in the window, but I couldn't stand any of them. Insects were bothersome, to everyone, as far as I could see – especially in cities where they served no beautiful purpose in caring for the flowers. At least in the countryside, you caught sight of bees busy about their work, keeping the gardens healthy. In the city, it felt like the bugs just plagued people and infested areas like maggots. I still never regretted leaving Fred's palace for a moment. I would have put up with anything, I thought, as I swatted the flies, one by one, with a tightly rolled-up newspaper. They fell to the sill, stunned, but I decided they didn't know anything about it. I wished humans could suffer as little as that in death. They didn't see it coming and their bodies probably didn't even produce any pain. They lived to torment people and died without suffering. In a way, it felt like I'd let them off easy.

I had to work that afternoon, preparing dinner plates, and catching up on all the dishes that had been used and discarded throughout the day. Whoever ate or cooked never took it upon themselves to clean their dishes. That was my job. I was getting paid to do it, so I knew that wasn't unfair, but I was getting peanuts as far as wages were concerned.

I was startled by a knock at my door. I had never received one before – any communication between myself and the other residents took place in the communal areas. The landlady didn't bother me either – so long as I was on time for work, and I paid my rent on time. So, I knew it was significant, but I didn't realise how significant until I opened the door. Daisy was standing there, smiling in a mocking fashion.

"Yes?"

"I just called over to say hi."

"Hi," I said, smiling.

"Can I come in?"

"Officially – no, but I won't tell anyone."

She walked in like she'd done the same thing a hundred times. She mightn't have been familiar with the specific room, but it could hardly be different to her own, and she was familiar with her own body. She had a certain ugliness about her, but it was strangely attractive. She embraced all elements of herself – even if they weren't desirable. I wished I could have that level of confidence. Mine had been knocked by my bad choices and I didn't trust myself anymore.

She lay next to me on the bed and pulled me close to her, so our cheeks touched, and I could feel her warm breath on my face. She kissed me and the way she did it was deep and all-consuming. I needed to come up for air, even though I'd wanted it to happen before the idea had probably even occurred to her.

"If we get caught, we'll get kicked out," I said.

"At least we'd be kicked out together," she said, breathily. She was talking straight into my ear – like she was telling me something secretive that bound us together.

The lamp was lit next to the bed and a moth fluttered in the lamplight, making dancing shadows on the wall.

"Don't you hate those?" I said, signalling with my eyes.

"Hate what?"

"All the bugs that live in here?"

"I don't pay much attention to them."

"How do you do that?"

"It's just nature, isn't it?"

I thought about how many things existed in nature that I didn't have natural feelings towards.

Daisy lay very still, talking at length about the workings of the moth, pointing out its fragile beauty, but she didn't sell it to me. I turned the lamp off when she stopped talking and it left, presumably. They always got frenzied in direct light where we could see them, and then vanished into the ether.

Daisy suggested staying in my bed for the night, but I knew it wasn't a good idea. Something could more easily go wrong if you were caught off guard, naïve in your sleep. She was forward and I liked that energy she had. It reminded me of my last real romance. I just hoped it wouldn't come to as abrupt an ending. It felt like everything in my life ended dramatically, and I was afraid of repeating that, so I sent her back to her own room. I softened the blow with a joke about myself. That's the Northern Irish go-to for a moment of discomfort: belittle yourself for someone else's good.

At breakfast the following morning, Daisy approached me as I was serving the food. There was porridge in a huge pot, and she dotted it on my cheeks, smiling affectionately at me. She didn't seem to be concerned about anyone else witnessing it. I liked her boldness. She didn't care about getting into trouble, or about what our peers might think. By comparison, I felt very uptight about everything. The act of being with her was making me doubt myself and doubt my own goodness. But I felt like I had turned a corner in my life, personally, and I wasn't prepared to give up my own liberty in exchange for Christly purity.

My hands were cracking terribly from being submerged in water all the time. Even washing dishes was hard labour then. There were so many old pans coated with burnt remains of past meals and nothing but a brush to tackle them with. You couldn't hope to get them all off when we didn't have the tools to do it. I used elbow grease, but they had been ruined long before I'd arrived. Nothing was ever replaced in the house. Household items were bought for life then – not until their shop-bought scent had worn off. I don't remember ever going shopping then. In Belfast, there were small independent shops and upmarket department stores, but I never had the money to spend in them and I didn't have the time to spend in them either.

I gave Daisy what I thought was the prettiest bowl for her breakfast and she winked at me. I noticed a few glances from the other tenants, but no one said anything. It wouldn't have occurred to anyone at that time that there might be something romantic between us. It was assumed that men were for women and women had sisterly relationships with other females, but nothing more than that. They must have thought we were like conjoined twins, with the amount of time we spent in such close quarters with one another.

The landlady was doing the rounds that day. She was in a foul mood. She inspected every dish I'd washed and demanded I rewash all of them. I felt like I was a slave to her, and she enjoyed having that hierarchy in place. Daisy told her to leave me alone and gave her a cutting look that the landlady met with silence. She didn't mention the status of Daisy's residency. I was relieved about that. Everyone ate ravenously that morning – there must have been something in the air. I was starving too, and I'd never been a breakfast person. I preferred to wait until I'd been up for a few hours before I started filling my stomach. I ate some porridge. It was plain and we never had anything to add to it – neither salt nor sugar, but I didn't mind. I was just happy to feel fed.

That day started more peacefully than it was meant to go on. An altercation occurred between two tenants and the landlady involved herself in it. She got a black eye and called the police. I didn't even know how it had started, but selfishly, I was glad it created a diversion from Daisy and me. The culpable tenants were removed from the building, but not charged with anything. The landlady wore her black eye with pride for several days. It was like a battle scar, showing how far she'd go to defend her territory. We knew not to cross her, but you could never predict who might move in next. With so many rooms squeezed together in the one house, disharmony was inevitable. There was something I much preferred about the sound of bickering to the sound of silence though. I knew I'd never choose to live in a quiet place again. When I thought of my previous place of residence, I didn't know how I'd ended up there. It might have looked different had my mother survived, but she hadn't. I didn't think of Fred often, or fondly, until he contacted me for the first time, at least. I got a letter in the mail initiating divorce proceedings. He was giving me a divorce and he was prepared to cover the costs, it said. I felt so grateful to him that it made me feel guilty too. He had been so reasonable, and I knew I didn't deserve that from him. I signed the papers straight away and returned them to him by post. The rest of my day looked up after that. I felt joy rising and expanding like lemonade fizz inside me. I was going to have true freedom again. I knew I'd likely have to go to court, but it was worth it. It felt like I was buying back my self-ownership.

I ran to tell Daisy. Her reaction to my news was somewhat disappointing. I'd expected a reaction of excitement, but she was just flat. Maybe my marital status meant nothing to her. I knew it was unclear what she was looking for in me, and I couldn't broach the subject. It had the potential to get too embarrassing, so I continued our ill-defined affair, enjoying what I could as it developed, and trying not to think too far ahead.

The two tenants that had been banished from the building were replaced overnight. Their replacements were pleasant, but they seemed to already know each other, so they kept to themselves. I never minded when people did that because it allowed us to do the same. The volume of dishes seemed to increase with their arrival. Some people just create more dishes than others and add to the stack of tasks you have to complete in your day. After breakfast, I cleared the table and started to scrub the bowls. Daisy walked up behind me, wrapped her arms around my waist and kissed me on the neck. I recoiled from her affection. I knew we might still have an audience if they'd happened to be looking in that direction at that moment. Daisy was always doing the things no one else would dare to do. She was rebellious. I'd thought of myself as being such, but in comparison to her I was quite biddable.

Daisy said she had something important to tell me. I was anxious about whatever she was going to disclose. She told me she'd got a job, modelling. I'd never met a model before. I could see how, cleaned up, she'd be photogenic, but I couldn't see her going to those lengths either. Overall, she was just a lazy person with a nice smile. She said she'd be taking a lot of photographs in Dublin. She'd have to get the train there, but they'd agreed to cover all expenses. I was trying not to let my disappointment show. I knew she'd probably relocate to Dublin. It didn't make sense for her to remain in the house. But I didn't want to discourage her either. There was so much tension between those two opposing feelings.

Daisy left a couple of days later to travel to Dublin. She invited me to go with her, but I couldn't afford to take the time off work. I wished her well and we had a drawn-out kiss goodbye. I was terrified it might be the last one, but I couldn't cling to her either. She had to do whatever she felt compelled to do. I knew our relationship could never amount to much anyway. We weren't living in a society that would acknowledge it, never mind approve of it. She was also making herself into an object for men, in posing for photographs. But I didn't share that opinion of mine. I knew I didn't have the right to comment on her life.

While she was gone, I noticed the other tenants. I'd expected myself to be miserable in her absence, but I was glad of some space. It felt like I was forgetting who I was with her there. She had a domineering type of personality and I wanted to always keep her happy. I was tiptoeing around her, I realised, but maybe everyone does that when they have strong feelings for someone, and the other person has the upper hand.

I washed dishes and I felt a sort of satisfaction in it, however repetitive it might be. I prided myself on earning my own wages, even though they couldn't cover more than my basic living costs. I still wanted to repay Fred, but I knew it would take me until the end of my life to do it. With the divorce proceedings underway, he'd be paying out even more for that. Fred was so well off he probably wouldn't have noticed the slightest change to his lifestyle after a big expenditure. Money wasn't important to him; he just had it. I wondered if he'd ever remarry. I knew the thought of it should make me feel envious on some level, but I regarded him as a brother. It seemed inconceivable to me then that I had willingly walked down the aisle with him. My parents' graves were close to his house, and I knew I'd probably never return to them. I hoped my parents wouldn't resent that, wherever their spirits lay. I knew my mother would show her usual unspoken understanding, but I didn't want them to feel their spirits weren't honoured by me – that they'd just been left to decay in the ground; even though that was inevitable whether I visited or not.

Betty, the landlady, was in terrible form that day. The interior of her bruise had turned from black to yellow. It was even more unsightly than the circle of black around it. It made my eyes water, looking her in the eyes. But she didn't seem to notice or care. I wondered how many black eyes she'd had in her time; probably many in her line of work. She had little control over who cohabited with her. Nor did any of us.

After I'd finished a long day's work, I retired to my bedroom. It looked untidy. My clothes were flung haphazardly around the room and there was dust on everything. I'd been so busy attending to other people's dirt that I'd had no time for my own. I was seeing how much I'd neglected myself and my own living quarters since knowing Daisy. We'd been spending far too much time together. I knew people must have suspected we were more than best friends, but at that time, there was a real naivety about those kinds of things. The house felt vacant without her there. It didn't matter how much of a clatter there was of the others going up and down stairs and hallways, hollering to each other, movements beneath me in the living room – I felt alone. When I was sitting in my bedroom, I looked at my bedside table and saw the battered Bible I'd been given as a child. I still kept it with me, even though I hadn't opened it in years. It was a big part of my childhood. I still could have recited many verses, word perfect. I wondered if Daisy had ever noticed it. I knew she was a complete atheist; not just an unbeliever – someone that hated any mention of the word "God." It didn't tally that she hadn't mentioned it to me – or that she hadn't laid eyes upon it.

The landlady was hanging around a lot that day, making sure everyone was doing what they were supposed to be doing. I took my break and then got on with more dishes. I knew every imperfection in every dish. Some had chips, others had line cracks running through them, dividing whatever picture was once painted on it. There was one of a beautiful woman, wearing a rose in her hair that had multiple fractures in it. It was one I always gravitated towards when I was serving dinner. Whilst I was working at my tasks, fear was looming in the backdrop. I was afraid that Daisy would decide not to return. I didn't even know if she'd left any of her possessions in her room. She could have settled her final bill without telling me. She knew about Emily. Maybe she didn't want to make me feel the same way. I knew I was thinking selfishly. I was more worried about losing her than I was happy for her to make her own way in the world. I was sure punishment awaited me for that; if not in my current realm, in another one. I sometimes thought about the afterlife. It was inescapable because of my upbringing. You can't fear something that greatly as a child and detach completely from it as an adult.

Religion wasn't relevant to my lifestyle, but the fear of it remained. I would always have Christian tendencies. They were too deeply implanted in me to completely rid myself of them. But I resented that too; Christianity condemned all my life choices – loving women, divorcing men, pursuing my own desires over faith. Knowing that something was wrong didn't mean I was capable of changing it. That applied to certain characteristics of mine that I disliked too.

I carried on with the monotonous tasks I had to do. They satisfied my hands, but not my mind. It wandered to Daisy repeatedly and I wondered who she was with and what she was doing. I felt anxious that she'd find something much better there. Dublin promised much more than Belfast, especially at that time. It didn't feel like anything exciting had ever occurred in Belfast and there was no draw about the place. It was before any of the trouble had kicked off too.

I was filled with anger and disgust, at the thought of how much I was devoting my headspace to her. I'd thought that leaving my marriage meant freedom, but there were always new binds you found yourself in. I refused to allow myself to fall into a position of enslavement again, in any form. I wanted to be as free as Daisy was – to have the freedom and independence of a bird. But I wanted to love her too. Her charisma overcame me, even in her absence. I replayed moments between us all day. But I didn't want to. I wanted to choose to think of more important things – in a general sense. In the scheme of things, one romance was worth little.

Betty was a hard taskmaster. She was getting worse the longer I was there. I knew I needed to spend more time away from the house. My whole life centred around it, and I didn't think it was healthy to spend such vast quantities of time in one spot. I felt the need to go further. Maybe I envied Daisy in a way because she'd had the opportunity to do that. I knew my looks would never carry me far. I was plain and I didn't have any feature that I thought was striking. Some people are blessed with many, but I was OK with not having any distractions from my mental world. I could blend into the background easily and be noticed as little as I wanted to be. It was useful sometimes - when I didn't feel like standing out. But it might have made a nice change to know what that was like too. I was satisfied with my looks, even if I wasn't often complimented on them – I was used to them and I accepted them. When I thought about Daisy and how loud she was in every way, I couldn't imagine her ever settling into the way of life I was happy to embrace.

The week passed languidly. I was hyper-aware of time, in a way I had never been before, even when I'd lived with Fred. That had been dull, hopeless time – not anxious, waiting time. I hadn't received any news of my own that week, which made it worse in a way. There was nothing other than labour to occupy myself with.

When the week finished, I was shocked when Daisy came to my door. She didn't arrive until long after dark, but she came to my door, like an eager dog dying for a walk. She had so much to tell me. I could see her eyes ready to burst with all the sights they'd taken in. Her animation awakened me too, even though my eyelids had previously been heavy with approaching sleep. I welcomed her into my room, and we sat, side by side on the bed where we'd made love countless times. I'd worried she was making something other than that – manipulation, or even a release of frustration, but her eyes told me it meant the same as it had to me. She talked ebulliently, telling me every insignificant detail, but it meant the world to me – that she took the time to do that. She'd travelled on the train to Dublin. It had been a longer journey than she'd ever taken before. People didn't tend to go as far then – especially from Belfast. It was the epicentre of people's lives there. They were accustomed to the same streets, the same faces, and the familiar greetings. They probably would have been uncomfortable with anything different. She'd looked out the window at all the passing countryside she'd never witnessed before, surprised by how green it was. She knew the island was famous for it, but she'd only ever been in the city, surrounded by bricks and concrete, trees that didn't contain the green that was characteristic of Irish hills. She'd needed different money when she got below the border and she had tried to familiarise herself with the coins on the way. It was strange to think that so many people had never laid their hands on British pounds, when she'd used them every day of her life (when she'd happened to have any.) Being rich was foreign to Daisy. She came from a working-class home, and everything was always hard for her family. She'd never got the chance to embark on an adventure before. But she said that she wished I had been there with her, to share the excitement. She wanted someone to turn to, to meet eyes with and recognise the same wonder at the new sights. I hadn't been to Dublin before either. She said along the way that the countryside was breathtakingly beautiful. The train was surprisingly busy, she said. More people took it than she'd ever been aware of. It was strange to think how open-ended so many lives were – with the potential for novelty on a weekly, or even daily basis.

When she arrived in Dublin, she was lost as soon as she got off the train. The station was busy, and everyone was walking confidently, like not one of them doubted where they were going to. It was a good time of the year to go, she said. Everything was blooming and the city was decorated with natural flowers. She was meant to meet someone outside the station. They had offered to take her to her accommodation. She'd just stayed in a hotel while she was there. She had photo shoots scheduled for every day of the week and she didn't know any of the locations, or how to get there. They said they'd arrange for taxis to pick her up. That was amazing to Daisy. She said she'd never set foot in a taxi before. There were so many conveniences and they acted like they were nothing special. Even without her make-up done, Daisy was striking, and she knew she was. I guess you needed to think like that to be able to step into that world. She told me about all the sights I wish I'd seen. She'd got a grand tour as part of her invitation. It was more like a calling. She drank beer in the local pub and tried and failed to read the Irish on the signs. She saw Trinity college and walked the streets, taking everything in. She said it felt like weeks without me. She enjoyed all of it, but she felt a strange pang too, that accompanied her for the entirety of her trip.

Her photo shoots weren't long and gruelling. She said they wrapped them up as quickly as possible due to the blustery weather. She was good at being captured in a shot with the exact expression they wanted to catch. It was ironic, I thought, considering how rebellious Daisy was with regards to everything else. She wasn't someone that did what she was told in life, but maybe the hefty payment was enough to induce her to. She said she felt rich, standing there. She just had to give a good photo in exchange for her money. It wasn't taxing and she liked the glamour of the photoshoots. Being outside had never bothered Daisy. She didn't mind being windswept and feeling awoken by the insistent breeze.

On her last night there, she'd been overcome by a strange melancholy. She went out for drinks with the rest of the photographic crew, but she said she was disengaged from it all. She spent the entire time sitting watching the glint of low light on a pint glass, like she was looking for meaning inside it, like a magic lamp. She vividly painted the scene for me, so I felt like I'd been watching her there. Apparently, she could hear the hum of the crowd surrounding her, but she wasn't part of it either. She was thinking about me, she said. It touched my heart to hear that. I'd thought with the independent creature she was that she wouldn't have spent one of her thoughts on me, especially with so much distraction around her. We were one and the same, I thought, in that moment.

Chapter Eight

Such peace rarely lasts, in my experience. That week, Daisy announced that she was moving to Dublin. It didn't make sense for her to remain in Belfast. She suggested I go with her, but I didn't see that as a positive thing. I was settled in my station, and I didn't know if I should stray far from it when I was in the middle of getting divorced. She hadn't considered that, but I could tell she was annoyed with me. That was when I saw the hard side to Daisy that I didn't like. She had a brutality inside her that came out when people didn't fit in with her plans. She was going to Dublin – that much was decided, but she thought I'd accompany her like a loyal dog, happy to be by her side without having any interests of my own. I knew that we were going to go our separate ways, and that made tears well in my eyes – just the prospect of it. In my mind's eye, I couldn't see that separation lasting anything beyond a few days, but in actuality, it would be permanent. Even the temporary version would have been hard to handle.

I knew I needed something to change in my life. It was torturous, watching the woman I loved moving on to other things. But it was worse, seeing myself, in contrast, sitting in the same spot I'd been in since leaving Fred. I'd been used to movement, even if I hadn't worried about big earnings or meeting huge goals. I wasn't used to staying in the same spot for years.

Daisy wanted my help before she left, and even though we weren't romantically involved, I still helped her. She'd been a close friend as well as a lover, and I couldn't just walk out of her life, like she was walking out of mine. She looked sentimental about the idea at times. She stared into my eyes, like she was trying to catch every last fleck of colour in them for the purpose of nostalgia.

Her bag was packed, and her room no longer had her mark on it. The landlady seemed relieved she was leaving. She was too spirited for her.

Tenants that are too spirited create too many problems for landlords. I knew she would be staying in an apartment that had been leased for her. It was central – adjacent to St Patrick's Park, she said. There was plenty of excitement unfolding around her. She loved being in the middle of the buzz. I wondered if she'd ever miss me, like she had on that short trip, and if she did, would I hear from her again?

I was at a moral impasse. I knew it was the best thing – for our union to end – in the eyes of the church and society. Not many people knew the truth about us. Being judged felt inherent to the whole thing, but it felt wrong for it to be broken too. We had slept together, and it disappointed me that I was beginning to leave a trail of broken bonds behind me. I knew that that part of it wouldn't bother Daisy. She was more progressive when it came to her views on that than I was. She didn't have that religious programming I did. I knew I had to rebuild everything. No matter how many times things were broken, I struggled to forgive myself. Each failure felt like another extension to a trail of smoke that followed my future movements. I could no longer freely move without condemnation, without visible regrets.

I knew I needed to take my thoughts captive, and so I leaned back towards my Christian upbringing again. Praying felt foreign to me. I only did it silently inside my head, so anyone else would have thought I was thinking average thoughts, rather than holy ones. But I hoped if I kept praying, I'd feel something – something that told me it was worthwhile – that they weren't just wasted thoughts going nowhere. I could remember that vividly as a child – taking the time to pray and not feeling anything in return. It was like I was shouting into a well and hearing nothing in return but the echoed notes of my own plaintive voice.

I didn't speak to anyone in my life about our ending. There wasn't anyone I could tell. I didn't even know how many of the lodgers knew about us. They had likely seen affection when we'd been together, but it could have been mistaken for something platonic. I didn't trust anyone else there enough to tell them anything personal. So, I kept cleaning my dishes, paying my rent and I tried to stay away from the place as much as I could in my free time. I walked the city streets. Even though no war was taking place at that moment – civil or otherwise, I felt something simmering below the surface of the streets. There was an undefined tension I could always feel. Maybe that was just because it lived inside me.

I was divided; torn between two halves of myself that didn't want to meet in the middle.

I didn't have any spare cash and there was nowhere to go to in those days, unless you had a lot of money. The department stores were for rare purchases – ones that had to be scrimped and saved for, for a year in advance – there was nothing immediate to buy. I felt like that was better in a way – it was simpler. Simple walks satisfied me. I got so much from them, visually and emotionally. It reminded me that life went on, even if it felt like mine was disintegrating in front of me. I walked into the corner shop, to treat myself to a bar of chocolate. When I entered the newsagent's, there was a spread of newspapers and magazines before me. I saw Daisy's face, fronting the magazine. It was a shock, even though I'd known that was what she was doing. It was like she was still watching me from afar, judging my progress. I turned away from it.

The man at the till asked me what was wrong, but I just said "nothing" and paid for my chocolate. He smiled at me, like he felt sorry for me, and I felt sad, thinking I inspired pity in people, rather than envy, or something more positive than that. I didn't want to see Daisy's face again. It had transformed before me from an object I loved into one I hated. She looked smug to me, in that photo, standing there with her hands outspread, leaning against one of Dublin's walls. I hoped she'd travel further then. It was strange that only days earlier, I practically would have begged her to stay, but by then I wished she'd move further afield, so I wouldn't have any more encounters with her face on magazine covers.

Everything was changing and I knew it was just a new phase. I was getting used to the cycles in life, but it felt like I spent more time at the bottom end than the top. I wanted that to change. I hoped if I returned to praying, I'd get some sort of return for it. I knew it was a selfish reason to pursue religion, but I supposed it was better than not doing it at all. I still thought about the afterlife and where I would end up. It didn't look promising. I had broken so many of the rules, and I hadn't followed Christ, crawling on my knees, apologising. In fact, I resented the thought of doing that. Maybe I was just always too stubborn to be a Christian. I tried but it seemed to always come back to the same point. So, I forgot it again.

People say you should place Jesus at the centre of your life, especially in Northern Ireland, and Christian cultures. There are a lot of people with extreme views, and they impose them on you too. I knew I was a disappointment. I needed something novel to do, to make it feel like I was living for a reason, rather than for paying rent in a grotty room. I needed a huge change.

That week, the final divorce papers came through. I didn't hesitate to sign them. I was so glad to get it done, and to post them. It felt much more important than my wedding day had. I read every one of the terms and conditions, few of them making any sense to me. It didn't matter; I couldn't find anything alarming in them. I knew that Fred was a decent guy and that he'd do his best for me, even if I had shown a lack of regard for his feelings. We had a court date to discuss the division of the assets. I hadn't planned on discussing the topic at all. I'd taken more than my fair share when I was with Fred and he didn't owe me anything, even if a contract said he did. The date was for a few weeks away. I had to appear in the courthouse, on the opposing side to Fred. I didn't like the idea of that. I didn't want to fight him, and I didn't know what to expect. It wasn't like I had a TV then and I could see a point of reference – some indication of what might happen, or the lay-out of the place. I knew that even if Daisy had been there, I would never have asked her to accompany me there. I suppose that showed how little I had trusted her, or how little I thought she would take my problems seriously. She was good for entertainment – not so much when you needed reinforcement in practical or emotional things. I knew in that moment that she'd been little more than a fling, whatever she called herself, or whatever she had told me she was posing as.

The weeks moved along, one merging with another, so I couldn't distinguish between the days. I was working seven days a week, so they were all the same. I wondered how haggard I looked. I felt like I must have looked exhausted, and I didn't want Fred to see me like that. I was meant to be flourishing in his absence. I'd have to face him, hopefully for the last time, in court that Friday. Even though he was a good person, and I knew he would cause me no trouble, the thought of it filled me with dread. I supposed no one looked forward to dealing with their divorce and the legal side just drew the whole thing out.

I walked into court as well cleaned up as I had the facilities to do. My clothing pieces were extremely limited. They'd been stitched and restitched to repair the holes. They never bothered me. I didn't stand out in the boarding house. But I minded that day. I went into the courtroom. I was wearing my best dress that I'd scrubbed thoroughly by hand that week. I'd got every stain out of it and my hands were bleeding, but it was worth it to me, to preserve my dignity.

I was ushered into the court room, and I didn't feel welcome there. The place had such an atmosphere of judgement. I was a woman, publicly getting a divorce at that time. The rest of the people in the room were all men. I felt their eyes upon me, but when I looked directly at one of them, he looked away, busying himself with something invisible in his hands. I was still unclear as to why I was there. There were no complications with our divorce – no children, no financial nastiness, no arguments.

The judge spoke first. He was speaking in legal jargon, and I couldn't make sense of much of it. Fred smiled at me from the other side of the room and gave me a wink. I didn't know what to do, so I smiled back and saved the wink. Why was he being so friendly towards me? I didn't deserve it. He was acting like we'd returned to the day before their wedding, as opposed to the day when everything was terminated. I wondered if he still loved me. Had he reduced me to the position of a fond acquaintance in his heart? I had no intention of keeping in touch with him, and that said nothing about his character. I thought very highly of him, but he had no place in my life and I didn't want him to stunt my future growth. The room had high vaulted ceilings, mahogany furnishings and no heating. It echoed so much that it felt like Fred's words were already haunting me. More than him as an individual, I was disturbed by how the situation reflected on me as a person. I felt terrible about the way it had all played out. I made a point of telling him that and he looked moved by it. I could see his eyes welling up with tears, but he composed himself. Then came the blow I hadn't seen coming.

"I want to leave half my money to Betsy" he said, shyly.

"She hasn't asked for anything – in fact, she's put in a request that you keep all of it. She won't touch a penny."

"That's why I want to give it to her. This woman was my wife – she's not a stranger to me. She deserves to have something. I want her to live a good life."

I shook my head and told Fred I couldn't take it. I thanked him profusely, but I could tell he was determined to get his way. He wasn't conceding to my refusal. I didn't want to feel like I owed him more than I already did. What I owed him was already a hell of a lot.

"Your Honour," I said, "I don't want to take any of it."

"That's up to your spouse," he said. I thought it was insensitive he called me that, as if we were still unified, but maybe the opposite would have been insensitive to Fred's feelings.

I didn't want any of his money. I didn't want him to encourage me to take anything. It was his hard earned and rightfully inherited money, and I wasn't entitled to it, as far as I was concerned. But Fred wasn't prepared to let it go. I left the courtroom significantly better off than I went in but feeling terrible about it. Some people show you more kindness than you deserve. I knew he felt happier knowing I had it, but I didn't want him to treat me like a charity case either. I already owed him too much. I knew he would be the only man I ever really trusted, but I still had to finish off my relationship with him. When I walked out of the courtroom, I knew we'd never see each other again – not on one solitary occasion - but I would always think of him with gratitude.

Chapter Nine

My life changed drastically after that day. I didn't live in the boarding house anymore. It was strange having money to my name, so I didn't spend it straight away. I wasn't used to being able to do that. But I knew I had to use it for good. I valued every penny of it, and I knew it was a gift I'd never get again. I had to do something meaningful with my existence. Tiding myself over in the boarding house had kept me happy until that point, but now that I had money and the means to do something important with it, it changed everything.

The day I left the boarding house was bittersweet. I told the landlady that I'd inherited money, but I didn't tell her the source of it. I wanted her to believe it had come from a kindly aunt, rather than my ex-husband. I didn't recall ever telling her I'd been married. We didn't discuss things as personal as that. Other people came from much baser backgrounds than mine, but I was still deeply ashamed of the failure of my marriage. It felt like I had failed personally on so many levels too. I packed up my belongings and told Betty that I wouldn't need my room any longer. She'd be keen to get it rented out on the same day I left, and it was strange – thinking that one day later someone else would have taken over my room and probably my job too. I'd washed enough dishes to last me a lifetime, but I hadn't minded it. If that had been my life for the rest of my days, I could have accepted it.

There was no one that was particularly sad to see me go. I'd spent time with the women, but it was mostly civil rather than amicable. The house was ever-changing anyway. New residents came and old ones left, and no one got particularly attached to anyone else. It was safest to keep it on that level. A large part of me wished I had done the same with Daisy. Then, her departure wouldn't have meant so much to me.

I considered throwing away my possessions. I had the financial ability to replace each one with a newer version, but I was sentimental about my harder days, and I wanted to keep reminders of them. I didn't want to throw away the things that had served me well for so many years. I'd been rich once before – by marriage, but even then, I hadn't lusted after anything pricey. I had to get an advisor to help me at the bank. I didn't understand anything about buying property or using anything other than notes and coins. I paid week to week until that point, and it was a completely different way of looking at the world – not having to do that.

I bought a large house. It was one of the old Victorian houses with many floors and bedrooms inside it. It was the kind of place that had been used for the boarding houses I was used to, but less delipidated. I knew it had probably been done up for the viewing, to win a buyer. Most of the changes were probably superficial, but everyone had problems with their houses then. Now, I've seen that when people have issues with their houses, they expect to get them fixed; but at that time, they had to work round them. No one had the money for repairs. The place was bright and cheerful. I felt my spirits lifting, just standing there, observing the cornicing and high ceilings. I could see myself there in my mind's eye; that's the best way to know you're choosing the right place. I envisaged what I would do with it. I had plans laid out in my mind and it was an adequate size to accommodate them. I needed to give something back to the community. Up until that point, I was ashamed of the way in which I'd lived. I felt like I'd taken so much and not given much back. I had been living in a selfish manner – trying to make it from one meal to the next, from one night's sleep to the next. But I knew I couldn't do anything truly selfish with the money. It didn't matter that Fred had forced it upon me. I would never think of it as my own. I wanted him to know I'd used it well. He mightn't ever find out, but I thought that on some level, he'd still know.

When I moved into the place, I didn't have any of my own furniture, but I quickly remedied that. I took one bedroom and made the kitchen and living room liveable first. Then, I worked on making the remaining rooms into bedrooms – each a copy of the last. They looked like blank canvases - décor wise. But that was intentional. They weren't for me, and I wanted people to put their own mark on them. I knew I would never have children, and I didn't feel saddened by that. But I needed to help someone – for my own peace of mind. There are givers and takers in life, and I felt like I'd unintentionally become a taker. I wasn't at peace with that. I still stood on the firm foundations of my Christian childhood, even without following the teachings as an adult.

I'd always been saddened by the thought of homeless souls wandering the streets, not knowing where to go for warmth. Some were lucky enough to temporarily stay with their families, but others had no one, and those were the people I wanted to help. I wanted to set up a free boarding house where the residents didn't have to worry about paying rent or bills. It would give them a safe spot to stay while they looked for work and rebuilt their lives. I hadn't heard of that before, but it was an idea that had been whispering inside me since I got the money. I felt a strong connection to people that looked lost. I'd never been entirely clear of where I was going either. I thought of how much of a relief it would have been, had I had the offer of a free room when I left Fred. So many people were living in poverty, and I wanted to help the ones that were the most misfortunate. Since the soup kitchen, I couldn't think of a charitable act I'd been in the position to do, and I wanted to alleviate that guilt. Even if I hadn't had the financial resources to do it, I knew I should have made time for people without getting paid to do it.

The place came together quickly. Having the funds to do it was an enormous help. I was good at looking after the basics by myself, but I couldn't have done the renovation works alone. Maybe it would have been different with an extra pair of hands, but it was an unthinkable mission. The place was huge and there was so much that needed done beneath the surface updates. We were lucky enough to have a shared bathroom inside. A lot of homes still had outdoor toilets then in Northern Ireland. I knew it was a luxury, even if it would be shared between ten people, and I appreciated it. I wanted to thank Fred, but I couldn't talk to him either. I hoped he would hear word of the place at some stage, and he'd know I had put his money to good use. It mattered to me – what he thought about me. He would have made a good husband, had I been that way inclined. I knew I was lucky to have met someone with so much love for me – even if it couldn't be reciprocated. Not many people got to experience that level of love in their lives.

I wondered what Daisy would make of my new venture, or if it would make me more appealing to her. She was leading an exciting life of glamour and I knew she probably thought I didn't fit in with that. Her face had become famous in both the North and South of Ireland – maybe even across the Irish sea. It was hard to avoid her image. Every time I saw a billboard or a magazine cover, her face seemed to grace it. I always felt like her eyes were staring into mine, like they could see me through the page. It's hard to avoid the eyes of the one you've loved even when they're no longer with you.

The house repairs were carried out by a team of workmen. They were skilled and they made it look functional but not unappealing. It took months to complete the work and during that time, the sounds of work taking place were the only noises I heard. I spoke to the workmen while they had their lunch or a cup of tea, but overall, I was alone. I had claimed my own bedroom and I had the chance to personalise it – something I'd never done before. It was strange having money at my disposal and not having to work my fingers to the bone to get it. I was happily retired from the working world. I hoped I could make my money last for a lifetime. I had no concept of how long it would last; I just knew there was plenty of it.

The builders finally moved out and I had the place to myself. It was completely hollow. Each time I closed a door, it sounded like the trap door snapping shut on the descent to hell. I couldn't bear it. It reminded me of the silent life I'd led at Fred's house. I was eager to fill the rooms, so I quickly went in search of tenants. I was dying to help someone, to ease my own conscience and to feel like my life hadn't been given to me for nothing. I knew my parents would have been proud of my venture. They'd always wanted to see me living independently, doing something worthwhile. They knew I wasn't made for married life.

The house was spooky at night-time. It was so dark, and I was sure I could sense the spirits of former occupants tarrying there. The house had fifty years of history and I knew a lot of things could have occurred in that time. I didn't think of the danger of welcoming anyone in. It just felt dangerous to me, being alone there. I was exposed to the ghosts that roamed the corridors, looking for a final resting place. It made me question my rejection of religion again. I could feel things that I'd thought couldn't exist. I worried about the state of my own soul and where it would end up when my time came too. I didn't feel like I'd done anything truly terrible, but that doesn't mean you've been a good person either.

I walked the streets of Belfast that day, looking for someone to approach. I knew they probably wouldn't want to stop and talk to me, but

I was wrong. Maybe they just weren't used to people initiating conversations with them. I found one man bundled up in a sleeping bag in an alleyway. He had a hat and gloves on, and he was so huddled up inside his sleeping bag that you couldn't see his face.

"Excuse me," I said. "Are you looking for a place to stay?"

"Aye, I'll stay in that shop front the night," he said, nodding at the entrance.

"I can offer you a room."

"I haven't got the money for one. If I did, I wouldn't be here."

"You don't have to pay for it – it's free."

"What's the catch?"

"There isn't one – I just want to help."

"Usually, things don't come that easy to me."

"I want to change that."

He did a laugh of disbelief. "You don't even know me."

He looked at me in a way that spoke of his suspicion of strangers. I knew it was probably a foreign concept to him – that I would help without repercussions. I'd seen how homeless people had been treated. They were shunned and left to their own devices. They usually stayed with someone, but if they'd made it onto the streets, they were labelled drunks and degenerates, and everyone gave them a wide berth. I didn't notice the odour of alcohol on him. He looked a lot more emotionally solid than I thought I would have been if I'd resided on the streets. Maybe it was just a front he had created to survive. I was sure he encountered more danger on a daily basis than I had in the entirety of my life.

"I know you don't know me, but I opened a home for people without homes. I thought maybe you could be the first person to stay there."

"I'd have to repay you somehow."

"You can when you've had time to sort out your life again."

He got to his feet and rubbed the aches in his legs. He must have been sitting in that spot for a very long time, or else the coldness was so intense it had frozen his limbs. He gathered up the sleeping bag and blankets he had. He didn't appear to have much else – no suitcase, and any of his important possessions seemed to be stored in the inner pocket of his coat. I couldn't wait for him to move in – to have my first tenant. It felt like the first good deed I'd had the chance to do, and I hoped it would be enough to redeem myself from the trespasses in my adult life.

"What's your name?" I asked him.

He looked like he'd have a nickname rather than a formal name, and he did: Billy.

"What's yours?" he asked.

I could see that he was already warming to me, and I wondered why. At first, he seemed unfriendly, but he'd quickly turned it around. At that moment, I realised he had a dog. It was small and it stood behind him, shaking from the cold. I took pity upon it too. I knew he should have mentioned the fact he had one to me, but maybe it didn't occur to him. The dog wasn't on a lead, but it instinctively followed him as we walked anyway. After a while, I reached down to carry it in my arms, but it growled and snapped at me. There was angry saliva spewing from its mouth. Maybe it only had affection for its owner. Maybe after what it had seen on the streets, it had to be that way. But I knew it didn't like me, even though, in a way, I was sparing it more suffering - maybe even saving its life.

Billy had such an overgrown beard that it was hard to tell what he looked like under it.

"Have you always had a beard?" I asked.

"Aye, I was born with one," he joked. "It's better that way – it saves you looking at my face."

"Do you need anything?"

"Like what?"

"Do you have anything to wash yourself with?" I asked.

"No, I don't own a toothbrush."

"Ok," I said, realising the extent of what I was taking on, but I didn't shy away from it either. The desire to help was so deeply rooted inside me.

I walked Billy to the nearest chemist's and got him the things he needed. He didn't seem to be embarrassed about asking for anything. But he'd had to exist in survival mode all the time; it was far more extreme than anything I'd endured. You couldn't be shy about grabbing money that was handed to you when you were in dire need of it. We left with several bags of items, and I felt a special warmth inside that I hadn't got to experience before. It felt better being on the giving end of things, rather than on the receiving end.

Billy followed me to the house. We probably made a strange pair. My clothes were no longer threadbare. They were simple, but they were clean and correct, and they didn't have holes in them. Billy needed a whole new wardrobe. In fact, he needed new everything. His teeth were rotten from years of neglect. He needed a haircut and a shave. It was hard to know where my responsibility for him ended and his responsibility for himself began. But I was prepared to do more than my share because I knew Fred had done the same for me.

It was strange having someone else in the house. Billy was a man of few words, but he was heavy footed, so you always knew someone else was there. I let him choose his bedroom. His eyes lit up at the sight of each one.

"How long is it since you slept in a bed?" I asked him.

"So long I can't remember what a mattress feels like," he said.

He smiled weakly then and I realised he did appreciate what I was doing – he was practised at not expressing emotion.

"I've slept in that sleeping bag for so long, it's all I know. I'll probably have to lay it on top of the mattress, to feel at home."

"Please don't," I laughed.

"Aye, it's dirty, isn't it?" he asked.

"Yes, but I'm sure it served its purpose. I won't force you to throw it out though. Maybe it could be a bed for Tommy?" I asked, looking at the dog, fondly.

It still gritted its teeth every time I made eye contact with it. I had a feeling we were never going to be friends, but I'd have to put up with him, for Billy's sake. It was strange feeling - like I was running my own boarding house, after years of being on the other side of that. I'd never have to pay rent again. That fact hadn't completely sunk in. It was surreal – going from having nothing to having money to burn overnight.

It wasn't long until our household grew. Billy knew a few people from the street. He told me where to find them, so we could invite them to move in too. The enterprise was proving more expensive than I had anticipated, but I hadn't considered the lack of belongings each resident would have. I provided meals there too. I resumed many of the kitchen duties I had carried out in the boarding house, but it was more rewarding – it felt like I was feeding the hungry and they needed it more than anyone else. I felt connected to the men that lived there, to how down and out they felt. We sat around together in the evenings. I made a big pot of tea, and they shared all their stories of woe with us. Some of them were horrific to hear, but it was a wake-up call. I thought I'd been through hard times, but I knew nothing of them in comparison to them. One of the men, called Jimmy, told us about where he sourced food when he had no money. He searched in the city waste, and he ate anything edible that he found there, no matter what it could have previously been touching. He didn't have the luxury of opting for packaged goods. He took everything that fell loosely between rubbish. Waste and food became one and the same thing for him, he said. He didn't eat for the taste or because he enjoyed it; it was purely for sustenance. A few of the others chimed in and told tales of the places they had got their food from. The stories were sickening. I had never been one to waste food, but I realised how lucky I'd been to be able to eat well at a table and to cook with fresh ingredients – no matter how simple they were.

It felt like people lived on bread then – bread, an Ulster fry, vegetable soup or some chips fried in fat. It was stodgy, but it was filling. I was sure my health was streets ahead of theirs. That was sad – considering the fact that I was likely older than most of them. No matter what I made, everyone devoured it. They were like circling birds of prey, waiting to descend as soon as food landed on the table. I quickly began to serve their food for them – to portion it into bowls or onto plates. It made it easier to control the amount of food we were using. Everyone always finished their food and there were no leftovers to be thrown away. I could cook all the simple Northern Irish meals well – champ, potato bread, soda, wheaten, stew. The guests were happy with my home cooking. It started off with a group of men that already knew each other. They seemed to have a secret street code I didn't understand. They were like close neighbours that had supported each other for years. Shortly after that, I found a woman to invite too.

When I was outside one night, I bumped into a pregnant lady. She was due in a short number of weeks, she said, and she had no roof to put over her, or her child's head. When I approached her, I expected her to posture like an animal ready for attack. She had that dishevelled look about her – her hair stood on end like she hadn't run a brush through it in months.

"How are you?" I asked her.

"Are you talking to me?" she said, surprised.

Her eyebrows looked startled, like she was preparing herself for a stoning. I felt sorry for her – that she had to live in such a vulnerable state on the streets.

"Where is your family?" I asked.

"Oh, they're all dead. I ran away from my husband."

"You did?"

"Yeah, he was a bully. Now he's dead, but I still have nowhere to go."

"How did he die, if you don't mind me asking?"

"In an accident in work. He worked in construction and was struck by something that fell from a crane."

"That's awful."

"It's better for me – having him dead. If he'd been alive, he would have dragged me home by the hair by now and punished me for leaving."

"Yes, I see what you mean."

I thought about karma and felt like it was real in that moment. It had been served to that bully of a man, but why hadn't the lady I was talking to ended up in a happier situation? At that time, unmarried mothers were something that inspired shock in the people of Belfast. They were so into godliness that they didn't believe in single parenthood. If a woman left her husband, it brought shame upon her, however he'd been treating her to cause her to leave. The man got to keep his pride intact, while the woman lost hers – she was branded a deserter like a man that had left the army mid-war. I wanted to take her under my wing. She'd developed a hard exterior. She had a broad accent and I thought she had probably acquired it for the purpose of self-protection. I wondered how long I would have survived, had I had her fate.

"I run a house for people without homes," I said.

I was finding out it was a difficult statement to make. It got people's backs up and they thought you meant something entirely different – like you were running a brothel or something. She looked at me, her head tilted to the side. I didn't know if she believed what I was saying, or if she thought it was just a trap. I was sure there were many traps set for people that lived on the streets, especially when they were women. It wasn't a time when women were particularly protected, outside of the gaze of a husband. The police didn't worry themselves much about the women they thought pursued alternative lifestyles and "chose" to live on the streets. It was sickening, but it was the norm then.

"Would you like to come and see it?" I asked. "I already have a few people living in it."

"Doesn't it cost a lot?"

"No, it's free. It was set up to help people put their lives back together."

"But why would you do that?"

"I don't have an agenda – I just have a house for people with bad luck."

She looked like she still didn't trust me, but she had the potential to miss out on something great if she walked away. She followed me, gingerly, like a cat on tiptoe. I didn't want to startle her, so I didn't talk unless she spoke to me first. My heart felt full, in a way it never had before – not even in a romantic situation.

She was waddling under the weight of the baby. I knew she could have gone into premature labour, from the harshness of her life, so it was especially important to protect her. Her clothes were filthy, and her face looked like it hadn't been cleaned in months. I wondered how on Earth she'd survived. Belfast was a small, safe city compared with anywhere else, but she was still the most vulnerable of society, sleeping on the streets. Anything could happen to you in your sleep when you're completely unguarded – even if you are someone strong.

We got to the house, and I knew she was hesitant about walking inside. It could have been anything – and once she was inside the door, it could have been bolted behind her. I knew her worries, like I could hear them playing out in my head too. I took her hand, and she didn't reject mine. She looked like she relaxed in that instant, for the first time in so long I couldn't even fathom. I led her through the garden. It was well-kept and it was obvious that it was cared for. The men that lived there had been keeping it in good condition for me. That was a kind of work they felt good doing. It gave them a sense of purpose, and I'd never learnt anything about gardening, so it worked out well. I'd had a garden landscaper come in before the house was finished. They had made some paths and seating areas, like little corners of paradise in an otherwise cruel world. I had seen some of the tenants using them and that filled me with joy. I'd even sat in them myself at times when I'd been wrestling with my own guilt and my own feelings of being indebted to Fred. I thought about my parents there and wished they'd been given a few more years with me. They were my only family, because I had refused the conventional kind of family I could have had.

I could see Edie's eyes brightening when she looked at the garden. She probably hadn't seen any pretty natural sights in a long time. The city was all red brick, factory smoke and footpaths. There might have been trees in small pockets, but none in other areas, and she had lived in one that lacked leafiness. I wondered about the power of trees and how they managed to transform an area. They lightened the air with their greenery and their air production. I knew I wanted to be surrounded by them for the rest of my days. Without them, things looked hopeless. The town was like a workhouse, turned inside out, so you saw all the ugly innards on the exterior.

"Do you know what you want to call the baby?" I asked her.

"Cynthia."

"How do you know it's a girl?"

"I just have a feeling she is. Do you have children?"

"No," I said. "I suppose having this house is the closest thing to having children that I'll have."

"You never know," she said, her eyebrows lifting suggestively. But she didn't know my thoughts on the subject.

"I feel like I belong here," she said, calmly observing the garden. "I could see myself sitting here peacefully."

"That's what I thought too," I smiled.

It was nice to have a female addition to the house. Even if I wasn't conventionally feminine, I appreciated being surrounded by female energy. There was something about Edie that reminded me of my mother's spirit, and the house felt closer to completion with her standing in the grounds. I led Edie to the room I thought suited her best. A few of the men passed us in the landing, and they gave her a second look. She nodded at them, but she didn't smile or say hello. Maybe she was worried about inviting trouble.

The room I had in mind for her had the best view. It overlooked the gardens so that in the summer, she'd get the benefit of watching the flowers blooming. I thought she could use the distraction of that with all that she had going on. She touched her stomach and jumped a little.

"The baby is kicking," she said. "I don't think I'll ever get used to that feeling."

"Do you not like it?"

"It's strange. I suppose it's like burping – it happens but I don't look forward to it."

"I've never heard it compared to burping," I laughed.

"I could compare my pregnancy to many unnatural things," said Edie.

I noticed then how weary she looked. She was hunched over, like her back was hurting and she was desperate for a seat. I told her to have a lie down and that I'd bring her some tea and something to eat. She nodded and didn't say anything, but I saw relief spreading across the surface of her strained face.

In the kitchen, I heated some barnbrack under the grill and slathered butter on it. The tea was hot and strong enough to stand up without a cup. I thought it would do her some good. Those seemed to be the things that the new residents always wanted when they were settling in. I would prepare a bath for her too. I had all the toiletries we needed in the house. I'd learnt after a couple of outings with the men that it was better to stock up than to take them shopping individually. That way, I could control how much I spent. In my experience, it seemed that the people that weren't used to having money spent it profligately when given half a chance.

I carried the tea to Edie on a tray. She was in bed when I entered and she looked like she was about to doze off, but she jumped awake when she heard me. It was like she was on hyper-alert the whole time she was sleeping. I felt sorry for her – that that was what rest had been for her. She was like a wild animal that had been rescued from the side of the road.

Edie politely thanked me for the tea, and I told her I'd prepare a bath for her and everything she needed. She said she only had one change of clothes in her bag and that she hadn't had a chance to wash them in months. I told her to strip down so I could clean them for her, and I gave her a dressing gown to put on. I knew it would probably need to be thrown out after one wear, but I was just happy to be able to improve her comfort.

The house had a funny feeling in it after Edie arrived. It felt like certain characters in it were lingering, trying to catch a glimpse of her. Maybe she was almost as vulnerable there as she was on the street. I knew I had to protect her. Just because the people I'd met were living in my house, it didn't mean I could trust them. We had built relationships with each other, and I knew their habits, but that didn't mean I knew what was in their hearts.

One of the men, Jack, I had since found out, had a serious drinking problem. I refused to pay for it, but he always seemed to find the money somewhere. I didn't know how he came upon it. He was more streetwise and resourceful than I had given him credit for. I'd just thought he was lost when I first encountered him. As it turned out, he was anything but. You could smell whiskey as soon as he walked into a room. I was sure the addiction was for a good reason, but I didn't know what to do about it. If he wanted to quit, he showed no signs of it. I didn't want to enrage him, especially with us sharing a roof, so I didn't mention the subject. He was quietly aggressive in his good moments, so I didn't want to do anything to knowingly aggravate him.

The others didn't have visible addictions. Or if they did, I was unfamiliar with their drug of choice. I didn't know how prevalent drug issues were in Belfast at that time. It wasn't a topic that was openly discussed. I'd never tried a drink. I'd never had the money for one, so I hadn't even sampled it. My parents weren't drinkers, coming from their ultra-religious backgrounds. They thought drinking was for working men's clubs and that it wasn't ladylike to partake in it. I didn't care about such archaic principles, but I never felt the desire to try it.

I filled a bath in front of the fireplace with boiled water. It steamed the mirror up. The steam swirled delicately through the air, like talented fingers performing touches of artistry. I knew Edie would be delighted to see the scene. I felt deep sorrow when I thought of what she'd been through, and I only knew the abridged version. I knew she was stoic too. I would probably never hear the unedited version. People that lived on the streets didn't talk; I'd learnt that. They might have done things I considered to be immoral in different ways, but they didn't share their deepest secrets, or anyone else's, for that matter. That was something I respected: their discretion.

When Edie was ready to bathe and the water would no longer scald her, I showed her into the living room. There was no lock on the door, but I made sure that everyone knew to keep out. There were a couple of men lurking in the hallway, so I sent them outside to tend to the garden. They looked less than thrilled. I didn't understand the appeal of a pregnant woman in the house. I thought that would have given her some sort of protection from the male gaze – like the child she carried wiped out her attractive features. But the men were curious about her. I knew they didn't regard me as a woman. I was too practical, and I set too many rules for them. I didn't dress in a way that defined my shape either. I enshrouded myself in baggy clothes that fell straight to the floor over whatever curves they might have seen.

I stood guard at the living room door, letting Edie wash at her leisure. She was already my favourite member of the household. I had no idea how to help with her pregnancy. In those days, it was mostly left up to nature. But I knew I'd need a nurse on hand when it came to the time of her labour. I had no experience in those matters and no one openly discussed them then. You were either practised in it, or you were completely ignorant about the matter.

When Edie left the living room, I was shocked to see just how dirty the bathwater was. Even the men's baths hadn't yielded the same amount of dirt. You couldn't see through the water. I wondered how healthy her child could be and it saddened me to think of the conditions of her pregnancy. It might have been an improvement having a roof over her head, but it still didn't feel like the ideal environment for a child. But she didn't seem completely unhappy with her lot in life. She must have known a lot worse, I thought.

I went out on my own to the corner shop. We were getting low on supplies. It was funny just how much food we could go through – with six of us in the house. There were still a few free rooms and I wanted to fill all of them, but I didn't want to empty my entire bank account to do it. I had to be sensible with my money, and plan for the future. There was a fine line between being kind and being stupid. I bought fresh vegetables, meat, household supplies, eggs and bread. I always got up at six in the morning to prepare breakfast for everyone. It was a satisfying start to the day. It took longer to do things like that then. I had a range and you had to tend the fire before you even thought about breakfast. As soon as the food was ready, everyone descended the stairs like hungry birds. They could sense when it was on the table.

One of the residents, whose name was Peter, insisted on saying Grace every time we sat down to eat. He was always very friendly and bubbly; Christ must have been at the root of it. I still didn't feel anything on a personal level, but I let him pray. It was a ritual of his, and those shouldn't be squashed, even if you don't believe in them. It was funny how accepting the others were of that. At first glance they appeared like they'd be cutting and make fun of him, but they never did. Later, I realised that that didn't necessarily mean they were good people; it just meant that they weren't bad in that particular way.

We were like a strange sort of family, because we always ate our meals together and we were joined in that one prayer. Even my own parents hadn't said Grace. It felt strangely mismatched with our unconventional living situation. But it gave the semblance of everything being safe. Maybe it made us all relax too much and feel like we could trust each other.

The first major disturbance arrived that week. Jack had been heavily drinking. I knew he was still meeting some of his old compatriots from the streets. He always came back intoxicated after that. I didn't feel like I could prevent him doing it. Just because he was living in my house, it didn't mean I could dictate whom he did and didn't see. I'd wanted to set up the house to provide people with his circumstances with a safe base from which to explore their freedom. I couldn't run against my own creation by laying down terms and conditions.

But that was the first time I experienced the bad things that came along with allowing that freedom. Jack was in a bad temper when he came home. I usually waited up for everyone. They didn't have their own keys to the house – that was the only security feature we had in the place. I couldn't risk having them arrive back with multiple friends to squat in their single rooms. I knew Jack was drunk before I opened the door. He hit the knocker ten times without leaving time for an answer. He was demanding and I knew he was ready to spit in my face. He had utter contempt for everyone once he'd had a drink, but I'd never seen him that bad before. I didn't know what he'd been consuming, but it must have been potent. I thought about the homeless people that drank any alcohol, drinkable or not, to get drunk, and I knew he might have been doing something similar. It was a kind of drunkenness that I'd never seen before: not just inebriation – something more sinister than that. I wondered if he needed a doctor when I looked him in the eyes. He was so far away inside them. It was like he'd given his body over to another force. He was ready for a fight with the first person he encountered.

"What have you been drinking?" I asked him.

He looked at me like he was contemplating ripping my head off. It was a terrifying look I never wanted to see again, so I shut up and moved aside. He stormed up the stairs and slammed his bedroom door. I hoped he'd stay in there until he'd slept it off. I retired to my own room. I could hear sounds throughout the night, but I decided it was best not to investigate them further. Some things were my business and others weren't. It sounded like a violent storm was taking place inside the house. I wouldn't have been surprised to open my door in the morning to find the rest of the house gone – flattened by the storm. No one else seemed to do anything about it either; I couldn't hear their voices anyway. I knew I'd have to brave the damage first. I opened my bedroom door the next morning, feeling less rested than I ever had before. The hall looked the same as it always did. I had to get on with making breakfast and I hoped everything would be restored to its natural state. I made a big pot of porridge, and the tenants made their way downstairs, one at a time, following the scent of my cooking.

Jack didn't make an appearance. I was sure he was nursing an unimaginable hangover in his room. I thought about checking on him, for his own safety, but I didn't know what mood I'd find him in. I never ventured into one of the bedrooms without the tenant's consent. They were charged with cleaning their own bedrooms since they were their own little private quarters.

As I spooned out porridge, a fly hastily knocked against the window. It was beating its head so hard you wouldn't have thought it could have survived it. But its head must have been harder than it looked. Maybe that reduced it to something robotic in my eyes too. I didn't think it had feelings – it just had a hard head it mindlessly bashed against the window. It had no concern for its own wellbeing either. I didn't think it cared whether it lived or died. I swatted it with the nearest magazine I could find. Its body was instantly squashed, and blood oozed out of it. But it didn't suffer. I'd stunned it so much it probably hadn't felt a thing. It was a kindness in a way – sparing it from repeatedly butting against the window, hurting its head to no good end. I forgot about it then. It felt like that small form of aggression was done for the benefit of the bug as much, as for mine.

I served so many bowls of porridge, all presented in different ways. Everyone had their own tastes – some liked theirs swimming in cold milk, while others liked theirs clumped together, some liked a sprinkle of salt – others a smattering of sugar. Every one of us was different – in ways that went far beyond our preferences in porridge.

Jack didn't show up until I'd cleared the breakfast dishes away. I was well underway with scrubbing them when he stumbled into the room. He still looked drunk, and he looked like he hadn't seen daylight in weeks. His eyes were encrusted with dried tears and his mouth looked like it was glued together with dried out saliva too. It was a sorry sight. I thought about offering him something to help, but I needed to remember that it was self-inflicted – it was something that he chose to do.

"Did anyone hear the racket during the night?" asked Peter.

Everyone nodded in unison and Jimmy piped up, "It was Jack. What were you doing to your room, mucker?"

Jack shook his head, stubbornly. He didn't look like he wanted to engage with anybody. I knew if I confronted him, he'd get nasty. He was obviously hungover, and in his book, that was probably much worse than being drunk and disorderly. He massaged his temples, like he hoped we'd all shut up if he rubbed them hard enough. I dreaded asking to see his room, but I knew I'd have to take a look at it. Like it or not, there were still ground rules. I couldn't keep someone in the house that was a danger to everyone else. Jack started sobbing. It took me aback. He didn't seem like the type for tears, over anything – especially over disturbing some neighbours he barely bothered with.

"I'm going to have to take a look at your room – can you give me the key?" I asked him.

I kept locking eyes with Jimmy, silently asking him to protect me from whatever outburst I might cause. My hands were trembling, but I kept them hidden under the table. It was important to never show weakness to someone as volatile as Jack. He looked like he was fuming with everyone. He drank his coffee loudly, like he was displaying his anger through the volume of his slurps. He didn't say a word and he didn't look me in the face. It was like I hadn't spoken. I tried to pull myself together for long enough to get to my feet and get the key. That was all I had to do, I told myself. I didn't have to achieve anything more than that – I just needed a key. It was a simple task – or it should have been. I stood, waiting for Jack to concede and pass me the key. I doubted whether he would. I fully expected him to keep me standing there until the end of our lives – in a face off that he'd never lose. I had to pretend to be tougher than him, even if I felt like I was melting like candle wax under the strength of his glare. He looked anywhere but at me, and I wondered why he wasn't trying harder to intimidate me. Maybe he felt outnumbered. He had a captive audience. Every pair of eyes was fixed on him, their mouths agape.

I held my hand out and I waited for him to slap it away. He reached into his pocket and set the key in my hand without a fight. It was surprising to me. He looked a little weaker then, like a balloon beginning to deflate. It felt like I was absorbing some of the escaped air. I was building myself up, reminding myself I was the owner of the house. It was easy to forget at times – especially when faced with a bully that was considerably larger than me.

I went upstairs. I expected to find something in his room, but I had no idea what. I turned the key in the lock and walked in promptly. It was worse than anything I could have imagined. The entire carpet was hidden beneath empty bottles of booze. But more worrying still, the furniture was overturned and damaged. It was clear to me that he had been throwing it around in a fit of rage. It upset me, seeing all the chipped shelves and doors – all the money I had invested in someone else's happiness, and he had rejected it in the most violent way. I couldn't bear to try to fix anything; there was too much to even contemplate. I stomped downstairs, ready to blow up at Jack. But he was sitting with his arms crossed at the table, completely relaxed.

"Jack, why did you destroy your room?" I asked.

"I didn't mean to – it was the drink – not me."

I was unbelievably angry with him. I wanted to lecture him about what it meant – the fact that I had used my inheritance to set up the whole enterprise so that he could have a roof over his head and a meal. Maybe his actions were because of the alcohol, but I was as angry as if he'd done it when he was sober. I knew he'd crossed a line I couldn't ignore. I didn't want to have a reputation for throwing residents out. They'd spent their lives being kicked out of places, in all likelihood - but what he'd done was beyond disrespectful, and he didn't even seem remorseful. I didn't decide anything in that moment. I took it away with me and played it out in my head. Jack wasn't likeable and he didn't get along with anyone in the house. I knew the house was filled with people with social problems and bad histories, but he was never going to follow a rule or try to make someone else feel less uncomfortable. I went away, seething for hours. I busied myself with cleaning the house and I told everyone else to stay away from me. They knew why I was in a bad mood, and I could see empathy in their eyes. That was something that people like Jack entirely lacked. He did everything on impulse, with no thought for the consequences and how they'd hurt others. After my rage had simmered down to deep resentment, I decided to broach the subject with Jack. I brought him into the kitchen while no one else was around and sat him down in front of a cup of tea. It felt inappropriate in a way – how hospitable I was making the scene look. I knew it could turn ugly in seconds.

"Jack, I need to talk to you about your room."

"I know, it's messy – it's not my fault."

"It's not just messy – you destroyed it last night."

"I've no recollection of that."

"But it did happen."

"OK, so what are you trying to say?"

"I'm evicting you from the house."

"But where will I go?" he asked.

His eyes got teary then, but I'd promised myself I wouldn't fall for it. I knew he was just turning on the waterworks. He'd never cried for anyone else. He was an opportunist, and I knew, in that moment, that not every homeless person was to be helped. That made me indescribably sad. It felt like it destroyed my faith in humanity – that one small act of destruction and disrespect.

When the tears didn't work on me, I could see Jack's anger rising to meet me instead.

"How dare you kick me out. You took me in so I wouldn't be on the street. You're a liar."

I tried not to rise to the bait. The only thing it would do was cause more destruction, so I quietly reiterated my point. Eventually, he looked disgusted that I hadn't reacted to his varying responses. He wasn't in control of me, like he'd thought he was. He forced his chair back from the table. Then he grabbed his undrunk tea and tipped it into the sink, so it sloshed up the sides of it and made a sprayed tea outside the sink too. It was like a last form of protest. But that was all he had left in him. I stayed put in the kitchen until after I'd heard him leave. He packed up his things and lugged his suitcase downstairs. I got up from the table then and opened the door that led onto the hallway. I saw him walking away, hunched over, his sleeping bag around his neck, dragging his suitcase behind him. It was a vision that would have inspired pity in many, had they not heard the full story.

That night was so much more peaceful, and it felt like everyone rested better. I knew I'd have to pay to have Jack's room fixed up before I found another occupant. I couldn't bear to look at it, so I didn't go inside again. I just hired someone to come in and look at it. Money was the quick answer to everything in those days, and it made me rely on others more than on myself. I knew it would have defeated me – tackling a mess of that magnitude, so it was easier to leave it to the professionals.

They managed to salvage most of the furniture. It just had to be reworked, sanded down and freshly painted. I still couldn't believe the audacity of Jack. It made me worry about the next occupant, when the time came that I was ready to seek out his replacement. Sometimes I quietly wondered what had happened to him after that. It still made me sad, thinking of him sleeping on the footpath, in shop doorways or in shelters with strangers with no scruples. But he was that type of person too, so maybe it suited him. A while later, I heard in the newspaper that a man had been found dead in the gutter. I instantly knew it was Jack. I just knew. They didn't publicise that type of thing then. If a drunk was found dead by his own doing, his death was swept away with the rubbish, never to be discussed again. But it had happened centrally, and his body was found in broad daylight, so it made it onto the news. Maybe there was nothing else interesting happening that day either and they were looking for scandal. I was just relieved that when he did pass on, it was months after I'd kicked him out and not days or weeks. I couldn't have carried the guilt of knowing that.

Chapter Ten

My illusion was shattered from that day onwards. I knew my money couldn't help everyone. There were people that chose to be homeless, through their need to fund their addiction, or because they didn't want a more stable life. I couldn't understand that way of thinking at all. But I was learning I couldn't change it. Some people didn't have a thick exterior you had to break through to reach the softness inside them; they just didn't have any of the softness to begin with.

Life was more peaceful for a time, apart from the repairs taking place. Our days were accompanied by the sounds of hammering. I didn't want to look at the room until it was finished. I told the workmen that. I wanted to see the final result – not the parts where everything was falling apart, and I could see the chaos caused by my former tenant. Sometimes I feared him. I knew he was a vindictive type of person. He wouldn't be staying far from the house, and it worried me that he still knew where it was. I imagined him following me through the streets and cornering me when I was least expecting it. I might have done him a favour, in taking him in, but that wasn't the part he would remember. I hoped he'd quit drinking, but I knew it was unlikely he would. He probably needed it to survive the kind of existence he had chosen. I knew the signs of an alcoholic to look out for in future, and I was grateful for that, at least. It was an education in a way of life I'd previously known nothing about.

Edie was heavily pregnant, and I knew I needed to protect her. I decided to put finding a new occupant for the room on hold until after she'd given birth. I didn't need to introduce an unknown into what felt like a safe setting at that stage. Everyone was pleasant to each other. We mightn't have known the yearnings of each other's hearts and our truest intentions, but we were able to be amicable at least. We always kept our bedroom doors locked from that point onwards. Jimmy was always talking about how lucky we were – as if we had escaped certain death. I knew it might have become like that, had I not removed him from the household.

Edie didn't seem anxious about giving birth, and I didn't know why. She didn't own anything for a baby yet and she didn't have the cash to be able to afford it. I took her shopping for the essentials. Maybe it gave her a certain amount of peace, knowing that I would help her to get what she needed. I'd come to view her belly as part of her personality – like she couldn't exist without it, but it was going to shrink soon. I hoped the baby would be safe in the house. It was a big improvement on their previous address, but I was on edge after what had happened with Jack.

I arranged for a nurse to move in temporarily. It would be costly, but it was worth it for our peace of mind. I knew Edie's labour was drawing close and I had no idea how to manage it. I knew she'd probably want me there for moral support, but I'd never experienced anything like that before. Edie told me she was having trouble sleeping and getting comfortable wherever she sat; she was ready to give birth and have full possession of her body again. I still saw the men in the house eyeing her at times, and I thought it was strange that they did at that time. Apparently, the fact she was female was enough to lure them in, even though she showed no interest in them whatsoever. She seemed to be comforted by the presence of the nurse. It helped having someone there that knew what they were doing. The extra bedroom came in useful for that. That was the first time I stopped to look at it. The workmen had done a good job with it. There was no visible sign of the destruction; in fact, it looked better than it had before the incident. The paints were fresh on the walls and the furnishings were made to match – a fresh coat of paint made them look like new pieces. I was glad I had somewhere pleasant to accommodate the nurse. I didn't know how many days she might be there for. Edie kept talking about giving birth, like she felt she would any moment, but the moment didn't seem to arrive. Maybe it's always like that when you're waiting for something. I'd grown as attached to the outcome as she was. I felt responsible for her wellbeing. She'd become like a child to me, even though there wasn't much of an age difference between us. I cherished her, but I never felt attracted to her. I didn't view her as being available to me. She'd been married to a man – and in a way, I felt like our failed marriages connected us more. Mine was incomparable to hers though. I felt such sympathy for her. She was very slight, and I didn't know how she'd had the bravery to survive alone on the streets. She was made of something strong beneath her apparent fragility.

I went out one day to get supplies from the shop. I knew that I needed lots of towels and blankets for the baby's arrival. We had a cot and a pram sitting ready. I knew some of the men weren't looking forward to the baby's cries, but they didn't talk about it when Edie was there. At least, in that way, the men that were there were considerate of others. I felt like apart from Jack, I had chosen well. But maybe I was wrong about that too.

Chapter Eleven

When I got back to the house that day, I found chaos. It was clear as soon as I walked in that Jimmy had taken advantage of my absence to corner Edie. She was resisting him and screaming, but no one else had come in. Maybe they were out, and they had no idea, or maybe they didn't want to involve themselves in the drama. I was shocked that it was Jimmy of all people. He'd always seemed like a gentle giant. But again, I was disappointed with what I learned. It felt like it was becoming a theme of my life. I couldn't believe that someone could stoop so low as to attack a woman on the point of giving birth. She was shaken, and rightly so. I didn't hesitate about calling the police. I called for the others to pin him down. They didn't know why they were doing it, but they quickly made sense of it once they saw his trousers open and Edie's dishevelment. With three of them sitting astride him, he couldn't attempt to move a muscle. It still felt like it took forty years for the police to make an appearance. I had the luck of having a phone. Had we not, I doubted anyone would ever pursue justice. It was scary to think of how many incidents might have been pushed aside due to that.

The police did eventually arrive, and the men did a good job of restraining him until they did. Jimmy was arrested immediately. There was less prevarication then about whose fault it was – it was clear cut. I couldn't look him in the face as he walked out of the room, and I knew he was trying to stare me down, to scare me and to warn me that I never should have involved the authorities. It felt like I had two people that wished me dead – that might even be soulless enough to make it happen. As the only witness, I knew they'd call me to testify, and that would only hurt me further. But I had to protect Edie at all costs. She was dependent on me, and I had made her that way.

After they took Jimmy away, I didn't feel any safer. Everything had become an unknown to us. It felt like anyone could turn on us at any moment. There were too many people in one house that had got by in life by grabbing onto passing opportunities. It was hard to know who had kept their values intact whilst living like that.

I tried to turn my attention to the preparations for the baby, but Edie kept bringing it up. She seemed haunted by the whole thing.

"I can't believe Jimmy did that. I thought we had an understanding."

"So did I. I know you weren't the best of friends, but I never thought he'd be capable of something so disgusting."

"I know, I don't want to be in the house on my own again."

"Did you feel safer before you came here?"

"In a way, yes – at least I knew to be on the lookout for constant danger."

The place of safety and goodwill that I had created was transforming into something else entirely, and I didn't want to face that fact.

Chapter Twelve

Baby Cynthia arrived that same night. Maybe it was the attack that sent Edie into labour; or maybe it would have happened naturally anyway. There's no way of knowing. I was awoken by Edie's screams. I knew the nurse was with her, but I still couldn't relax. They were gut-wrenching screams, and I couldn't bear to hear her suffering. I stayed in the hallway, unable to rest, never mind sleep, waiting for the arduous labour to end. The nurse kept everything private, and I didn't get a glimpse of the room. I was curious, but I didn't want to see the gore I imagined on the other side of the door either.

I was called in after she'd been cleaned up. Edie was holding Mary and she looked so proud. I wondered what it was that wiped the rebellious spirit out of any mother immediately after giving birth. She looked softer and happy. It was strange she'd been in such pain only moments before and she seemed to have already forgotten about it. I couldn't imagine her staying in the house any longer then. It just didn't feel like the right place for her, but she had no other options.

The nurse looked happy and tired, but she reassured me she'd stay up throughout the night with Edie. It was funny how she seemed to understand the dynamic we had, when I would have struggled to explain it to anyone in my own words. Edie offered the baby to me. I'd never held a baby before and I was afraid I'd drop her, or that she'd start bawling the second she was set in my arms. But she just lay quietly staring at a fixed point in the distance. She was immediately loveable, and I knew she'd become another member of my family.

But after the birth, everything changed between Edie and me. She was distracted and I was absorbed by Cynthia too. It was as if she was my own child and it felt like Edie and I were working at cross purposes. Things settled down for a while. But they say bad things always happen in threes. And in that case, the saying was right. I'd never believed in superstitions like that, until it happened. I thought we were almost like a family: Edie, Cynthia and me. Maybe I was just delusional in thinking that. We did everything together for a long time. Edie wanted my company. She seemed to crave it more since giving birth. Maybe she was desperate for adult conversation, or she just didn't want to face parenting alone. We went for long walks with the pram. I knew that wasn't the reason she was living there. She was there to rehabilitate her life and I was making it too easy for her. But I felt a tenderness I couldn't suppress, and I wanted to ease her problems. Sometimes I thought she'd been sent to me, like a special assignment – someone to bless with good things.

Not everyone in the house was inactive. There were tenants there that worked hard to change their circumstances. I understood why they wanted to better themselves. It must have been difficult to share a house for that length of time, with people you wouldn't necessarily have chosen to be close to. But the surroundings were beautiful and always well kept. It wasn't like they were stuck in squalor. Their relations with each other were the main thing that caused trouble. Why, when you put a large group of people together, do they never seem to gel? They just rub each other up the wrong way, one way or another. Even if two people are getting along famously, there are always another two squabbling like siblings. It was always like that. It was hard to find peace, but that was what I was there for – it was my calling in life – to smooth it all out.

But I couldn't have anticipated the thing that would make me unable to endure it a second longer. The house was empty after the nurse left, so I took on a new tenant. I found him myself, at the side of the road. He looked to be in a sorry state, but I knew I would have been the same in those circumstances. I had to shake him to get him to come round – he was in such a deep sleep. I knew it wasn't from alcohol. There was no smell on his breath. He just looked cold and close to death. My heart expanded as I saw him, and I felt tears warm my face. He looked like he'd given up on trying to live any longer and I wanted to save him.

"Excuse me," I said, shaking him, harder and harder, the longer it took him to respond.

He held his hand up in protest, but his eyelids were very heavy. I persisted until he came around. He was noticeably shivering, even though he was bundled up in several coats and a sleeping bag. It looked like everyone else was just stepping over and around him. It wasn't fair – having to live like that and being judged on top of it. He had a hat sitting in front of him, but there was only one piece of change in it. I picked it up and gave it to him.

"Come with me and you can get warmed up."

He didn't even resist my invitation. His body seemed to find the energy it needed to follow me. I knew the doctor would need to see him, but he seemed scared by the idea of even meeting with one. I didn't want to traumatise him or scare him away, so I didn't push it. We fell into walking at the same pace. It felt like we had an unspoken understanding between us. I knew he was like an animal that could be easily scared away. I didn't want to be the thing that made him jump. It took us a while to get to the house and I could see how weary he was. He mustn't have eaten in a long time. His cheeks were drawn and looking at them made me feel like I'd spent a lifetime being spoilt with every luxury. Simplicity didn't look bad when you compared it to starvation and suffering.

When we got to the house, he looked breathless – physically and mentally. I didn't think he'd ever observed something so decadent before or felt so deprived by contrast. He'd soon have his own room, but he didn't know that yet. He thought we were just having a cup of tea or something else as fleeting as that. I was nobody to him, then.

When we got inside, Cynthia was crying. She was hungry and seemed to be distressed day and night. I thought she was also upset by the nurse's departure. However small she was, I knew she must have been aware of the dramatic change. She'd spent lots of her time being nursed by her. She must have felt like another maternal figure to her. She had several of them in her life, but no paternal one. When I heard her crying, I wanted to come up with a quick solution, but I knew that I couldn't do that. It was something that only time could change.

Jeff looked shell-shocked when we walked inside. Maybe he associated loud noises with bad things. I couldn't control the noise levels for his comfort. In a large house, that wasn't an option, with or without the presence of a baby. He winced at the sound, but he didn't comment on it. He just gave me a tired smile when I looked him in the eyes. His eyes were yellowed and watery. I didn't know what had turned them that colour. I knew people that drank too much usually had that feature, but I didn't attribute it to that. I could just tell that he wasn't a drinker. There wasn't a hint of it about him, and I'd already experienced living with one. I knew the signs by then, even if I'd been ignorant of them earlier.

I led him into the living room and invited him to sit wherever he liked. No one else was in the room and it was flooded with Winter sun. It made it seem like it was a hotter day than it really was. It was bitter outside. I noticed he was still shivering, even though we were sitting in front of the lit fire, the sun and fire making heat together like we were on the surface of the sun. It was a sad sight. He was such a big man, but he looked really frail. I wanted to ask what had happened to him, but he seemed private too, so I didn't bother.

"Can I get you a cup of tea?" I asked.

"I'd love that," he said. He didn't look me in the face, like he thought he was a lesser being than I was.

"And then I'll fill the bath for you and leave you in privacy to get warmed up."

"Why would you help me like that?"

"If you're expecting a catch, there isn't one."

"I've never been shown kindness without one."

"Maybe you're due some."

"How do I know I won't have to repay you in some way?"

"I don't know how to promise you that. I just thought it might be better than where you're living now."

"I'm used to it – at least I know it."

"It's heart-breaking to watch though. I thought you were about to pass away."

"It felt like I was, but the street is my home. Good or bad – I'm used to it."

"So do you not want to stay here?"

"I wouldn't turn down a room. I know I was about to die where I was living. It was so cold."

Then he narrowed his eyes at me. "Who else lives here?" he asked, conspiratorially.

"I have a few tenants from similar situations."

"So, you picked them up on the street?"

He seemed to have forgotten about his cup of tea and it was tipping forwards in his hand, threatening spillage on the carpet. I righted it for him.

"Yes, they are all people that are building their lives again. You'd have that in common."

"I'm not here to make friends," he said. "Trust no one – that's what I've learnt."

"So, you can't trust me?"

"You can't do anything to me that hasn't already been done," he said, simply.

I could feel my eyes pooling with tears, so strong was my empathy for him. He looked so lost and drawn in the face. His cheeks were as sunken as two empty pockets. I wanted to reach out and touch his face. I wondered how long it had been since he'd had any sort of real human touch. Still, I knew not to do it. He'd flinch like a scared animal – then he'd transform into a fox on the run. I'd probably never see him again and always wonder what had happened to him.

Even though he didn't trust me, and his defensiveness was the first thing you noticed about him, there was something endearing about him too. It was like I could see the child in him: the one that had existed before all the damage was done. Then I thought about the fact that he wasn't all that different to me; we were all damaged as adults in our own ways.

I waited for him to finish his tea. Once he remembered it was in his shaky hand, he drank it in one long gulp and then set it delicately on the table. He looked like he was afraid to break or scratch anything.

"Don't worry," I said. "I'm not precious about things. This house was built to be lived in."

"I just don't want to disrespect you," he said. "I know I'm suspicious of everyone, but I get a good feeling about you."

I showed him to his room, and he was delighted with it. It was like watching a deprived child receiving all their desired Christmas presents at once. He looked like he came back to life when he walked into his own space. It was weird to put someone else in the room. It had been the nurse's room and I still hadn't fully accepted that she had left her post. It felt like I was left with the responsibility that she had set down on her way out the door. But I'd always had it, and it gave me a sense of purpose. The room was plain and painted in what were then considered unisex colours. I could easily adapt it to whomever decided to move in. I wasn't sure that Jeff had accepted my invitation yet. Even though he looked interested in every aspect of it and his demeanour had changed, he seemed like one of those tenants that would be a continual flight risk. You never knew what he was really thinking. At the time, I thought that added an interesting layer of mystery to his every expression. But I didn't know the risks associated with that depth of mystery.

Chapter Thirteen

I was spending a lot of time with Jeff. Edie seemed jealous. I still had time for her and Cynthia, but it wasn't as concentrated as it had been before. Jeff had so much he needed to sort out, from the moment he walked into my life – even the very basics. He looked like a chastised child when I told him to bathe himself. Maybe he just wasn't used to the concept of bathing freely. Water costed a lot for the homeless people I had met; they rarely had access to it – especially in the quantities required for personal hygiene. When Jeff met the others, I could tell that they feared him, but I didn't know why or what exactly it was that communicated that to me.

When I drained the bath water, I couldn't believe the filth in it. The water was brown, and sediment sank to the bottom of the tub. It would have been disgusting to most, but such things didn't bother me. I thought that I must have had the makings of a nurse inside me. I'd always felt such an urge to care for everyone and I was putting it to the best use I could, without the prospect of ever having my own children. You don't have to have children to be maternal.

Still, it felt like I did have a child when I cared for Cynthia. She always beamed when I came into the room, and she seemed to immediately calm down. Edie was doing a good job with her, but I knew that she was unlikely to ever move out. She didn't have the ability to manage working and paying bills alongside raising a child that was her constant companion. Maybe no one could have managed it at that time. I thought I'd be lost if she did move out, so it suited me for her to remain in stasis. But she didn't seem entirely happy either. I felt like she wanted me to fill in as a dad to her child, but without any of the benefits associated with it. She didn't show me much affection. It felt like we were rapidly drifting apart after Jeff arrived. I had more to attend to in life than just Edie, but I didn't think she saw it that way.

I knew I was absorbed by Jeff. It wasn't intentional – he just demanded a lot of my time. He was a confusing cocktail of self-involvement and self-effacement. I could see that he was getting stronger, the longer he stayed with me. It was satisfying, watching someone repairing their broken life, but there was something slightly different about his rehabilitation. I couldn't quite put my finger on what it was, but something gave me a bad feeling in the pit of my stomach.

That week, there was some disturbance in the house. Jeff had an argument with one of the other men. They had started with a simple dispute over food, and it had escalated into something else entirely. Maybe it was just a means of channelling their anger. I tried my best to keep them apart, but I didn't want to get between their fists either. Those were the times when I thought I should have found a partner with whom to start the charity; to deal with the physical aspects of it.

There were raised voices most days in the house. I hated experiencing that kind of polluted atmosphere – destroyed by bad tones and foul words. It affected everyone in the household, even if they were safely hidden inside their own rooms. I didn't know why bringing Jeff into the house was bringing me so much trouble. He'd seemed like a quiet soul when we had first met – as fragile as a mauled bird. I didn't want to make sudden movements around him in case he fled. But it was becoming apparent to me that he was much more competent than I'd thought. He was good at controlling people through his own behaviour. Maybe street life necessitated that, but it was unpleasant to live with.

Peter cornered me one day and asked if I was going to have him evicted.

"No, the thought never crossed my mind," I said. "I couldn't do that when he hasn't broken the rules."

"He's a troublemaker."

"I know you have a personality clash."

"It isn't that."

"I need you to do your best to live peaceably with him – for everyone else's sake. I don't need any grief. There's enough to worry about in the household without having to worry about that."

He rolled his eyes at me and looked at me like he thought me completely ineffectual. I felt powerless too. It felt like the house I was meant to run was running me. It was a charitable organisation that was becoming a constant source of stress to me. On the rare occasion I took the time to look at my reflection in the mirror, I immediately noticed the aging on my face. Worry had made lines like little roadmaps all over me. Youth had been stolen from me, but I knew that was something I was bound to sacrifice in exchange for the organisation I wanted to have. You couldn't run something like that without it taking its toll on you.

After that conversation, things worsened, but I found it hard to pinpoint where the issues were coming from. They involved everyone in the house, and it felt like everything was descending into chaos. I awoke to the sound of doors slamming and screaming. There were fights in the hallways: ones I had to break up. I'd even received a few scratches and bruises myself. It felt like the house was a dangerous place to be – like an extension of the streets the characters living there had formerly resided on.

Not long after his arrival, Jeff found himself a girlfriend. He never took the time to ask me whether I minded her visiting. He invited her over like it was his own home. I remember the first day I saw her there. I was taken aback because I'd never seen an unfamiliar face in the building before. She was exceptionally friendly, which made it harder in a way. I wanted to show her my unfriendly face, but she wasn't going to allow that. She was bubbly and chatty and I didn't know how to respond to it. It makes it harder to deny someone access to your house when they greet you warmly. But she had a cunning look in her eye too. It told me she wasn't pleasant in a naïve way; she knew the workings of the world. I supposed she would have to - to pair up with someone like Jeff. He seemed indifferent to her presence. He carried on with his day as if she wasn't there at all. It was a puzzle to me, how they'd even had the initial introductory conversation that helped them connect with one another. Siobhan must have taken full responsibility for it, I thought. Jeff was just there for the ride. Now that I'd seen him cleaned up and with more confidence, I could see what was appealing about him. He was a person that had a certain draw about them. You wanted to get to the bottom of what made him who he was. It was like something you had to solve, or you'd lose sleep over it. Even though Siobhan was so pleasant on that first encounter, it felt like she propelled everything towards the breakdown that soon followed.

Some people are just a bad influence on others. It was just a rotten combination when she and Jeff got together. On the surface, everything seemed perfectly kosher, but behind the closed door of their room, I knew strange things were going on. I never tried to enter it. There was an air that surrounded the place that acted like a repellent. I wouldn't have even knocked on the door with clean sheets or to offer anything helpful. It was like there was a red mark on the door, keeping me well back. It was no longer an area of my house that belonged to me. I didn't understand the exact set-up. Siobhan didn't strike me as someone that needed bailing out from her circumstances. She was wise and I doubted she'd ever spent a night on the street. But she was the type of person you knew never to say no to. She wore thick make-up, especially for that time in Northern Ireland. During that phase, lipstick might have been worn and a hint of brown eye shadow, but she was always wearing a heavy palette and she wasn't embarrassed to stand out. It made one word spring to mind when I looked at her: audacious. She had to be that way to live rent-free in my house for the homeless, I supposed.

Jeff was always in terrible form. Whatever hope I'd seen flickering in his eyes had been snuffed out again. He seemed like he was in a bad mental place. I knew he wasn't a drinker. He grimaced if you even mentioned alcohol in his presence. He said he'd grown up with a father that drank a lot and it had put him off for life. He couldn't even stand the smell of it; never mind the taste. But he didn't seem like he was "all there." His eyes were far away, like they'd been taken elsewhere by a substance. I knew nothing about substances other than alcohol. As far as I knew, they were impossible to source at that time; they weren't even a consideration in daily life. Northern Ireland was so far behind everywhere else then. The look of the place was enough to show you that. There were grand, old buildings, but the insides of them were uninspiring. You could walk around the city for hours and never find anything to do. I doubted that anyone would ever have the desire to come to Belfast from elsewhere. In my mind, it was a dull place with little to offer, and the people I lived with had seen the absolute worst of it. I knew they had a right to feel disillusioned. I put Jeff's feelings down to that – his string of disappointments.

I thought that everything would be tranquil after Cynthia was born. That had been the main thing causing me concern for months, and it had finally passed us by, and we were still standing. But that was the least of it. Sometimes it's easier to direct your worry into a specific goal, instead of letting it expand into a worry that covers every possible outcome. I should have been worried all along, in a general sense, but that was a lot for one mind to cope with. It was easier to deny the risks associated with my organisation. I wanted to see the best in people; to believe that they were trying to make better of themselves, but I didn't consider the fact that there were so many that had no desire to do that. Jeff was a rule breaker. No matter where he'd gone to in life, I knew that he would never go along with whatever was asked of him. I was beginning to understand how he had ended up living on the streets in the first place. At least the house was expansive enough to contain all of us without us having to be like tinned sardines. That was the one saving grace. Jeff and Siobhan passed most of their time in his bedroom. Even though it concerned me – what they might be doing in there – it was better for the other residents that they were offside. I thought that, quietly to myself, but I didn't realise the extent to which that was true until the drama began to unfold.

There was more and more movement in the building. It was hard to keep track of it all because there were several exits and entrances. I knew that if a resident so wished, they could easily carry out a double life and no one would ever find out. It was the kind of layout that facilitated sneakiness and secrecy. I knew there were more people in the house than there had ever been before. They mightn't have stayed as permanent tenants, but there was constant traffic passing through. I couldn't work out what it meant, but my gut knew it was something bad.

Edie looked like she was tiptoeing around, trying not to step on the eggshells left by other members of the household. She was sad and uncomfortable. Her baby was always with her. She didn't leave her unattended in her bedroom for a second. There might have been locks on the doors, but it felt like the people there had the means to pick every lock, to do things that I'd never learnt about in my comparatively sheltered life. I knew I was out of my depth, but it was too late to turn back. It was like I had waded out into the depths of the Atlantic, and then realised the true power of the tide and currents too late. I could never get out again. My body succumbed to whatever nature had in mind for me. It was the same in the house.

Sometimes, if I got a chance to see Edie in private, I wanted to divulge everything: all my worries and fears, all my concerns about Jeff. But it felt like there was a new wall built between us. I knew Edie resented me for welcoming him into the house. In her view, that bedroom had belonged to her dear nurse, and it was meant to remain empty, like a shrine to her and the birth and everything enormous that had happened since Cynthia had arrived. I understood her feelings about that, and I didn't judge her. Sometimes I expected Peter to barge into the room and kick Jeff and Siobhan out. He was well-built, and he had a certain aura. Even I knew when I shouldn't cross him. He could be vicious if he wanted to be. Maybe everyone that has stayed on the street overnight develops that tendency.

I didn't want to know what they were up to. It was easier to turn my head the other direction and act like everything was moving along without any glitches. But it was hard to avoid noticing strange details because they were so loud. I never saw them apart anymore and they even took their meals to their room. I might have been able to corner one of them individually and question them on what was taking place, but as a pair, they weren't to be tackled. They knew how to keep my questions at bay and how to work the other tenants, so they could create the ideal circumstances for themselves.

I waited weeks and weeks for my chance to come – a chance to talk to either Jeff or Siobhan alone. Finally, it came by surprise. I walked into the kitchen one morning and Siobhan was making two cups of tea – one for herself, I presumed, and one for her literal partner in crime. She didn't say hello and I didn't say it to her either. Her usual smile was missing, and she had bad energy swirling around her. I could feel the darkness of it engulfing the room. She stirred the tea viciously – like she was trying to get all the life out of something that had once irritated her.

"Can we talk for a minute?" I asked, hesitantly.

"What about?" she said.

She was eating something crunchy, and she smacked her lips together when she talked. Her every move just screamed to me of disrespect for me and my home. She didn't even need to be there, and that made me very angry. She might have been sharing a room, but I felt that she was using resources that were designed for other people. She was making a joke of me – taking my food, helping herself to whatever crockery she needed, sleeping in a bed built for one person.

"Your status in this house," I said, tentatively.

I was afraid of talking too loudly in case I said the wrong thing and I couldn't take it back. It was strange how approachable she looked, and how unwelcoming her eyes were. On first impression, she looked like one of those fun, colourful types that accepts everyone and everything, but that couldn't have been farther from the truth.

"You're not happy that I'm staying there?" she barked, defensively. Evil came into her eyes and tainted the blue of them. They were so light they reminded me of the sea on one of its colourless days. They lulled you into a false sense of security in their natural state. Maybe they were part of her game – they were meant to hypnotise you and distract you from whatever she was doing. I didn't know what it was, but I knew I didn't like it. I wanted her to leave the house and I was ready to ask her to. I'd had weeks of annoyance building up in my system and it was time for it to be released.

"I'd rather you left," I said, abruptly. It was better to keep it short, if not sweet.

She was incredibly volatile, and I could sense the anger deepening inside her, like a bull lowering its head before the chase.

"It's not up to you," she said. "Jeff invited me to stay."

"But it's my house and what I say goes," I said.

I sounded unconvincing, even to myself. She looked at me with a smirk and then gave a little rasp of laughter. I felt mocked and I was ready to return to keeping my distance from her. She didn't even dignify my answer with a response. She just grabbed her cups and went upstairs to the bedroom. I no longer imagined it to be like a simple hotel room. I knew it was something else entirely. I dreaded to think what kind of hovel was on the other side of that door. I decided it would be better to talk to Jeff. Physically, he might have been broader and taller, but I couldn't imagine anyone being as manipulative as Siobhan.

I dared to knock on the door. I'd never done it before. Up until that moment, I could never find the courage to. But I had righteous anger in that instant, and I was going to direct it where it belonged before it burned up inside me. I kept banging the door and waiting. I wasn't going to give up until I'd seen the contents of the room. I mentally prepared myself to face a putrid mess, or worse. I ran all the worst scenarios through my mind at once. I didn't expect them to answer the door. I'd never seen them open it for anyone other than each other. Even when they slipped inside, they had a way of doing it that shielded the contents from anyone on the other side of the door. Finally, Jeff opened it. He looked at me through two slits of eyes. He looked like he'd just woken up from something deeper than sleep. He could have told me he'd come back from the dead and it would have been a believable statement.

The room was pristine. I'd never experienced such clattering disharmony before, between what I expected and what I found. They looked like they were living in better conditions than the rest of the household. There was something almost boudoir-like about the bedroom. They had changed the bedsheets to their own plush ones, rather than the generic ones I gave to each occupant of the house. They were a deep red, reminiscent of blood, and it changed the whole look of the room. I knew I should mention it. If they were able to afford luxuries like that, it felt wrong that they were staying in the room at all. But I didn't know how much money Siobhan had. She could have been incredibly wealthy for all I knew, but without her, Jeff had nothing. It was a difficult position to be in. I couldn't throw one out without the other, but I knew only one of them was entitled to live there.

"When did you redecorate?" I asked.

I backed away a little as I did, expecting a backlash. But Siobhan just smiled at me – that sweet as sugar smile that made me feel like I'd over-indulged.

"Do you like it?" she asked.

There was no inflection at the end of the sentence, so it didn't sound at all like a question at all. It was a statement to shut me up: a way of fobbing me off.

"I can't say I do," I said. "But at least you're keeping the place in good nick."

"Yes, we make the best use of the space we have," said Siobhan with pride. I wondered why she wasn't bashful when she said that. Had the situation been reversed, I would have been horribly embarrassed. But evidently, she wasn't the type of person to experience feelings like that.

There was nothing more to see in the room. In a way, it was disappointing, to not have an immediate answer to whatever strange situation existed within. I knew there was something; I just didn't know what it was. They didn't bother with any of the rest of us in the house. They just stayed in their tower, descending only for the things they needed to take - meals, supplies, favours. I'd never had such a strongly negative feeling about someone nice before. Siobhan was nice, but she wasn't. Her eyes didn't match her smile and when I thought of them, they spooked me. It was strange to see such an evil contrast between a smile and the contents of her eyes. I thought about the expression "the eyes are the windows to the soul," and I thought how true it was. I didn't like the view of her soul I was able to glimpse from the outside. Jeff was different too. He didn't seem like the poor, vulnerable victim I'd met. He had become something else: something strong and determined to thrive, at any cost.

I realised then how hard it was to determine when someone was fit to stand on their own two feet. People took advantage of your hospitality – at least, the ones that were opportunists did. It was sad to think how many of them there were on the streets, waiting for a place to stay and for someone to pay for them. They had no intention of ever working or making something better of their lives. It was disgusting when I thought of it like that. I'd approached certain homeless people, thinking they were to be pitied in their current state, but maybe they just saw me walking towards them like a blank cheque on legs. It was sad to think of someone using another person in such a calculated way, but maybe I was guilty of doing it myself and I was receiving my deserved punishment. I knew what I owed, and I would pay it, whatever it costed me. I knew the money I'd funded it all with wasn't mine. I saw it as a loan I could only repay through good works, so I had to stay patient. I couldn't evict another person without good reason to do so. Having a hunch about something wasn't the same thing as having concrete evidence for someone's misconduct.

I left them alone to do whatever they'd previously been doing and went downstairs. Edie was crying and the house had a general bad mood to it. I knew I needed to get away from it for a while, so I decided to go and buy food. Walking down the street alone, hearing my own thoughts felt like a treat. I realised how long it was since I'd had room for them in my head. I was so preoccupied with other people's problems.

After that day, I decided I needed to take things a little less seriously. I was always emotionally involving myself in everything that was happening around me. I needed to detach from it and allow the tenants to take care of themselves. I had provided them with a safe space in which to do that, and that was enough – or it should have been. People tend to take as much as you give them and if you give too much, they don't even feel the need to say thank you.

Chapter Fourteen

After a period of relative peace, I realised things were getting off kilter again. Edie had had enough. She was threatening to leave every single day. Part of me hoped she would because I couldn't bear to listen to it anymore. She kept talking about it, but she didn't make the move to leave. I knew why she wanted out. It was a strange place to live in long term. But I knew it also must have been easy to get too settled and to feel like you couldn't move on again.

The noises from upstairs got stranger and stranger. There were groans and screams and I knew something sick was going on there. I didn't know whom it involved or what exactly was happening, but it was frightening. The residents all seemed restless. They were in constant motion, never taking the time to sit or sleep in the house. It was becoming untenable, but I didn't know why. The men that lived in the house were leaving, one by one. They were suddenly highly motivated to rebuild their lives. They hadn't been in as much of a hurry up until that point, so I knew they were feeling pushed out of the house, but no one would tell me exactly why.

When I asked Peter about his departure, he was very secretive about it. He didn't give me a forwarding address and he had no desire to stay in touch. He told me he wanted to start from scratch and make a new life for himself. His face looked brighter when he talked about the prospect of leaving. I knew in my heart that I wanted to leave too, but that would have been purely for selfish reasons. I couldn't follow those. I was leading a life of service for the rest of my days on Earth.

Edie was speaking to me less and less. She barely came out of her room anymore, and her appetite seemed to have waned. She used to stay in the kitchen for a large proportion of the day, eating meals or awaiting the next one, but she had no interest in food anymore. I didn't see much of Cynthia either. I could hear her crying when she was unhappy, and the rest of the time, there was an uncomfortable silence. It felt like all the rooms had been vacated; all but mine and Edie's. That was when I realised, the tenants provided me with as much comfort as I did them. I felt safer, knowing they were there – the ones I'd known for years, at least. I was familiar with their ways, and they were with mine. You could get used to most things if you put up with them for long enough, but not the behaviours of some – no matter how discrete they tried to be about them.

I had a feeling something bad was going to happen in my home. I could feel it like sharks sense the movements of edible sea life approaching. I didn't have anyone to confide in anymore. Edie was nowhere to be found. She left before I awoke and returned after dark, as far as I could tell. I had several empty rooms, just sitting, waiting for new occupants, but I didn't have the will to fill them. That would have required me to walk the streets, looking for new residents, and I didn't want to do that. It felt too risky. How was I meant to know what someone's intentions were? I couldn't know that. I realised how trusting I had initially been. I might have thought I knew a lot about life then, but I really didn't. I was unguarded and people had seen how exposed I was.

I thought about closing the doors to the place, but it was too much in opposition with what I had promised myself. I couldn't allow inconvenience or personal difficulty to detract from what I was doing. I had a duty to society. It was the only way to redeem myself. I thought back to my Christian upbringing with immense guilt, and I thought of all the values that had been imparted to me – that I had actively chosen not to follow. I couldn't fake the faith, but I knew if I didn't, punishment awaited me on the next plain. I had to become a better version of myself. Sometimes, I thought my parents were regarding me from their position in the sky, judging what I was doing. I knew they would have been disgusted that I'd inherited money from Fred. They wouldn't have judged me for leaving, but I should have made my own way in the world – I thought that, and I knew they would have too. I hoped they were happy with what I was doing with my time. Their opinion meant a lot to me. They'd been my caregivers and providers and that had created an everlasting bond. I needed to have their approval, so I wondered why the tenants in the house didn't feel the same way about me. Soon, the only ones that were left were Edie and Jeff.

There were sordid happenings in that bedroom. I knew it without having to look in. It didn't matter how perfect it appeared on the surface.

It was an easy place to lead a secret life. There were various alternative exits and entrances, so they could come and go as they pleased, without being observed. Edie was in the room beneath theirs and she told me she had trouble sleeping at night because of all the noise. It was impossible to say what it was; the noises were just bumps that could have been caused by any number of things. I wanted to ask Edie more about them, but she only told me the bare minimum then. It was like she didn't trust me anymore. She thought I was no longer an ally of hers.

I put up with the strange atmosphere for as long as was humanly possible, and then I barged into the upper bedroom one day. I was surprised to find it unlocked. Both Jeff and Siobhan were inside it, apparently still in bed at two o'clock. I didn't know how they could stay holed up in there for so long, without tiring of each other or of their meaningless existence. As soon as I walked in, I knew from their faces that I'd made a grave error. They didn't like anyone on their patch – especially the person that owned it. The curtains were still drawn, and the bed was unmade, but everything looked like it was in order. There was no mess to complain about. There was just an "off" feeling. I had to find out what was creating it, even if it was in a way that could be considered dishonourable. I knew my tenants had rights – if not legally, then at least morally. But those rights tied in with however much they followed the rules. If they were breaking the most basic of rules, how could I allow them their full freedom?

I waited until night time and I stationed myself beside the back door. I had an unshakeable feeling that that was their entry. Whatever it was that they were involved in, they were doing it via a back entrance. The place was so sizeable that anything could have been taking place without my knowledge. I crept downstairs. I didn't want to be visible, but it felt unavoidable. There was nowhere I could place myself without being seen. But if they passed that way, I knew I had the right to intercept whatever they were doing. It would be clear to me that it was against my rules.

I waited all evening. I had made myself a pot of tea and I hoped the caffeine would sustain me until the moment of revelation arrived. The room I sat in was just a spare space – like a scullery-turned storage cupboard. We kept all the cleaning equipment in there, but other than that, there was no reason to be inside it. I brought a wicker chair into the room, so I had somewhere to sit while I awaited whatever mystery was about to be revealed to me – I hoped. It took hours, but I didn't get bored. I was too wakeful, needing to know what was happening in my house. The hours moved in cycles that didn't matter to me. I could have sat there for days, or weeks. My curiosity was finally satisfied when the door opened. It wasn't locked. I rarely locked any of the outer doors, so I didn't have to liberally dispense keys. They knew they were onto a good thing. Siobhan walked in first. She was chirpily chatting. It was surprising she didn't try to lower her voice one bit. She was brazen – more so than I had even realised. She didn't even jump when she saw me. She just looked me straight in the eyes, without shame. Jeff followed her into the room. He was holding the hand of another lady. She was wearing revealing clothes. They were skin-tight and her cleavage was exaggerated by her bra, which was also exposed. It was clear to me what her profession was. Jeff looked completely at ease with her. I didn't understand how they could afford her. It seemed like she was a shared commodity. She didn't look like she knew the house. It must have been here first time there because she looked like she was waiting to be led to the next room.

"Who are you?" I asked her, directly.

She looked at me, with her mouth open, waiting for someone else to put the answer into it for her.

"This is Colette," said Jeff. He didn't expand on how he was associated with Colette.

"You know you aren't allowed guests in the house," I said.

"She isn't a guest," he replied. He clutched her hand and tried to walk away from me.

"Get out of my house," I said to Colette.

She looked at me with eyes as clear as crystal balls. She didn't have an ounce of embarrassment in them, and I knew she wasn't going to leave. She'd probably never followed a rule in her life. They were well matched – the three of them – in their sociopathic tendencies. I dreaded to think what might go on in the room once she was there.

I reached out and grabbed Colette's arm, pulling her back towards the door.

"You can't stay here," I said.

"If you don't let me, you'll be sorry," she said, in her deep, rich voice.

She intimidated me, but I didn't want to be frightened in my own home. I was still in charge, whether it felt like it or not. I told her to get out and I pretended her threat didn't scare me.

"I'll call the police if you don't leave," I said.

She let Jeff's hand drop and stormed towards the door. As she passed me, she spat in my direction. I pretended not to notice. She left and the others glared at me. I had scuppered their plans for the evening. I felt proud of myself for having achieved that. Maybe it wasn't a huge achievement, but in the boarding house I was running, it felt like it was. It wasn't just that I had prevented something immoral happening in my home – I had exerted myself and demanded respect from my tenants. It felt like it had taken far too long to get to that point. I was wrong though – to think that I had arrived at the final scene. There was much more to come – but it was better that I didn't know that then, and that I got to bask in the glory of thinking that everything was resolved.

Chapter Fifteen

Edie announced that she was leaving. I was heartbroken, but I didn't let it show. I was shielding my feelings from her because she was already so guarded with me. I didn't feel like I knew her anymore. It was strange how quickly you could become unacquainted with someone you'd once known so well. I didn't know why she blamed me for whatever was occurring in the house. Maybe she didn't trust me anymore – to protect her, or to put her first. Whatever the reason, she didn't explain herself. She just announced her departure in its decided state. There were no further arrangements to be made. She had Cynthia bundled up and ready to go. She only had one bag that contained all their worldly possessions. That made me so sad. She was leaving with little more than she'd arrived with – including the baby. She was so distant that she wouldn't look me in the face. I didn't understand what had created such discord between us. We'd gone from being exceptionally close to being far apart, even living under the same roof.

I offered to carry her bag to the door, but she refused. I had only one room filled at that point, besides my own. It was a strange feeling, knowing that there were so many sitting vacant. I was afraid to invite anyone else to stay, until the current problem was resolved, and I didn't see any resolution on the horizon. Since the night when I'd managed to eject Colette from the house, there had been nothing but trouble. Instead of accepting my regulations, they had upped the ante with the guests and their illegal activities. I was tempted to call the police in, but I knew how hard it was to evict someone. Once they were over the threshold, there was no turning back, unless you managed to get an order to remove them. To do that, I'd probably need solid evidence of their misbehaviour, and I didn't have that. I didn't even own a camera then. There was no trail left behind them, and the only witness was leaving. I knew I couldn't rely on her to back me up anymore. We were no longer in the same camp. I told

Edie to wait before she exited the door. She gave me a look that told me she despised me, but still, I moved towards her and kissed her tenderly on the cheek.

"You're always welcome to come back here," I said.

"No, I'm not. I'm not welcome here now."

"That isn't the case," I said.

"You don't know the half of it," she said, bitterly.

"I wish you'd reconsider, but I can't force you to stay either."

"I've been a prisoner here for long enough. It's not a normal environment."

"I'd agree with that, but it will all change soon."

"No, it won't – you don't have the will to get rid of him and his harem."

"I don't think I'd describe it as that."

"Well, what would you describe it as?"

"Dysfunction."

"That's a joke. Why does he have more rights than me?"

"He doesn't. He's just more forceful about exerting his. I will get him out – mark my words."

"I won't be here to see it when it happens. Things have happened that I won't even share with you."

"Why not?"

"Because you're ineffectual – as a landlady and as a protector."

I shook my head and I felt so deflated when she said that. It had been my life's purpose – protecting others. She was so angry with me, and I'd never wanted to create that feeling in her. She was my beloved, even if I'd never been able to adequately articulate that to her, or to anyone. I was unclear on whether it was romantic, platonic, or sisterly love, but I knew without a doubt that it was love.

When she walked out the door, I felt like the gentlest part of my personality died. She took it with her, and she didn't even know she possessed it. I wished I could follow her, but I was tied to the house. I felt that if I left the place unsupervised for so much as a day, I'd return to find myself evicted. It didn't matter whose money paid the bills when you have someone as bold as that living with you. I knew that Siobhan thought she had more rights than I did. She just saw me as a weak woman. Maybe I was – I thought. I'd always thought I had a more masculine strength running through me, but in the face of such evil, I felt like it had been reduced to nothing.

I called Edie's name, gently. I tried to raise my voice, but nothing came. I was the only person hearing her name in that room. She'd never know that I had called her back, that I'd wanted to stop her. I felt like running after her and begging, but I knew it was no good. Whatever I had failed to do, she wouldn't forgive me for it then.

That night, I could feel a huge shift in the atmosphere of the house. Any goodness that had been left in it was gone. I missed the sound of Cynthia's cry, even though I'd always hated to hear her cry. The place was soulless. The top floor was occupied, with God knew what, but the rest of the rooms sat empty. I was desperate for someone to exchange a few words with – even meaningless pleasantries. I wanted to make dinner in the largest pot I had – the one I'd used when we had a full house. It was tucked away in the back of a cupboard – with no need to come out again any time soon. I needed to get rid of the current problem first, or rather, to find the strength first to do it.

I waited and took my time. I was going to pounce, but I needed to wait for the right moment. I hadn't seen anyone else entering the building that day, even though I knew it happened daily. They had some sort of strange business going on up there. I knew about prostitution, and that it was one of life's sad realities, but I suspected there was more to it than that. The women came in looking different than when they walked out. They usually had bright red, tear-stained faces. They always pretended I wasn't there – that I couldn't see them passing me. It was like they were ghosts belonging to another realm – ones that had left their humanity behind them in that room. Siobhan and Jeff seemed to get stronger daily. When I did see them, I sidestepped them. They had a real violence in the way they walked around and spoke. I'd never seen something as seedy as that before. I couldn't even give it a name. They were such a strange couple. I'd never seen them kiss, but they somehow seemed romantic with each other. Maybe they just shared the same depravity and that created a sort of sick bond.

I'd always liked the room they shared. It felt like I secretly reserved it for special people. The rafters affected the shape of it, and it was more like a tiny apartment than a bedroom. I knew then that I'd made a mistake in giving it to Jeff. I should have moved Edie into it instead. They thought they were above reproach. Every time I thought of Siobhan with her perfect face, I felt nauseous. It stood in opposition to everything she was as a person. They were louder than ever. At first, they'd made some attempt to minimise the noise, but once they knew I was aware of some of their activities, there was no longer a need to cover them up.

One night, I phoned the police. I knew as soon as I started speaking that they didn't want to know what I had to say. I was female, after all. At that time, it felt like the word "female" was synonymous with over-reacting, emotional outbursts, and general hysteria. You weren't taken seriously about serious matters. I expressed myself as rationally as I could, but it made no difference. I knew the man on the other end of the phone wasn't really listening. He was making all the right noises, but he didn't sound engaged. I knew they wouldn't come out – or if they did – they wouldn't search the house or examine the activities there. They probably just thought I was a crazed, late-night caller – someone whose bad dream had affected their perceptions when they woke up.

"What has happened tonight, madam?" he asked.

I didn't know what to say. Nothing specific had happened that day. That was all they were interested in: immediate crime. I knew it was likely to be happening, but I didn't have the words to define it either. I hung up without bothering to say goodbye. I didn't want a stern talking to, or a condescending remark. I didn't have the patience to endure it without snapping. I knew I had to set a trap of my own, but I couldn't think of a way out. I wished I could call on Fred and ask for help. He was the one person I could truly rely on to help me out, but he'd already done too much, and I'd created my problems with my own two hands. He'd invested in them without even knowing it. I was too ashamed to speak to him. We hadn't exchanged a word since the division of assets. It was better that way, I supposed. I didn't want to hurt him further. He was a good soul. I doubted that I was the same. I might have started out with good intentions, but everything was falling apart around me. I wished I could walk out and never return to the house, but I had to be responsible. I knew if I walked away from the home, I would never have the chance again to redeem myself. I didn't know for sure in whose eyes I was trying to. Did I believe in a god that watched my every move and decided upon my eternal fate? I couldn't say I did, but I couldn't say I was an unbeliever either. It was still instilled in me.

That day, as I sat in my room, I became aware of a spider marching across the floor. It felt like the final straw. I'd always hated creepy crawlies in every form, and I didn't want it to invade my house too. I grabbed a newspaper, rolled it up and flattened it in one swift whack. I lifted it with the paper to make sure that it was dead. The legs had disengaged from the body, and it was clearly lifeless. I went to get a dustpan and brush, so I could dispose of it. I knew that some people disagreed with treating insects like that. I could remember a Sunday school teacher I'd had once, harping on about God's creatures and how they should all be treated fairly. I just thought they were a nuisance. I wasn't sure of the purpose they served, other than to annoy people. I didn't feel sad when I removed the carcass from my room. I was glad to know it was gone and that it could no longer make its way across my space. One type of home invasion had been ruled out.

There were more bumps than usual that night. I could hear every single one, even though my bedroom wasn't directly below theirs. I couldn't sleep. I hoped I would catch them doing something illegal, so I had real evidence. They seemed too smart for that, but arrogance often took over and pushed common sense down. I ran into Siobhan in the hallway. She was carrying a plate of food, overloaded to the point it looked like it would feed five. Maybe that was what its purpose was. She looked me directly in the eye and I felt like she was threatening me. I didn't say a word to her. I just waited while she ascended the second staircase. I was still waiting for a disclosure. Maybe it would all get too much for her – the guilt that must have been her constant companion – but it never did. I doubted in the end that it had ever existed inside her. That was what enabled her to live as she did, using and mistreating others.

I stayed at the bottom of the stairs, waiting for Siobhan to open the bedroom door. But she knew I was there, and finally she turned and glared at me. I knew she was trying to intimidate me, so I didn't try to enter again. I wouldn't have knocked on the door, but I would try to grab whatever opportunity I could to see inside the room. I waited day and night, unable to sleep. I never seemed to leave that old scullery. After a few days I'd move to a different door, hoping I wouldn't miss anything. They might have changed their route, dependent on where I was stationed. They were slick. I knew they wouldn't fall into the same trap twice. After days of monitoring their movements as quietly as I could, I noted that they tended to leave together in the early evening and reappeared thirty minutes later with a new scantily dressed acquaintance. I took my next chance and hoped they wouldn't return early for an unpredictable reason. I waited for a few minutes and watched them through the window. Siobhan turned back and met my glance. She knew I was watching their every move. She wasn't stupid enough to miss that. Either they were setting me up or they were just barefaced in their actions. I let the curtain drop from my hand and I knew that Siobhan would be happy she'd scared me off. It was a little victory for her – another chance for her to exert her position at the top of the house.

I raced upstairs and kicked the door open. I knew I didn't have a minute to waste. There must have been evidence of something – however small. There had to be with so much coming and going and so many visitors. I hoped for something substantial – like fabric with blood on it. It mightn't immediately be clear why it was there, but it was indisputable evidence. The look of the room surprised me again. The bedsheets had been freshly made, the floor was gleaming and there were no strange objects sitting out. I opened the drawers and the wardrobe, but there was nothing amiss – just clothes hanging there sadly - an assemblage of interchangeable men's outfits.

There was nothing else in the room. It was as if it was a hotel room, stripped and emptied for the next occupant. I didn't understand where they had hidden their stuff. You could tell just by looking at Siobhan that she was a materialistic person. She liked fine jewellery and things that sparkled and enhanced, or rather, supported her beauty. There wasn't a single piece of it lying around. Maybe she always took it away with her because she didn't trust anyone in the house – or more specifically, me. I had run out of places to look, but I kept going anyway. I overturned everything. My mind told me that there had to be something. I couldn't just accept that nothing was amiss.

I gave up and righted the things I had knocked over. I wasn't in a rush to go downstairs, but I made myself do it anyway. They would be back soon, and I didn't want an argument. We still had to live together, after all. We'd almost established an agreement between us: if I let them do what they wanted, they wouldn't intimidate me in my own home. When I thought of it like that, it was blackmail. I needed to get them out of the house, but it was proving more difficult than I ever could have imagined.

They were great at covering their tracks. I knew that Siobhan must have been more capable than Jeff. Sometimes I pictured him as he was when I met him. He had transformed into something else overnight. Maybe I had too. There was a sensitivity inside me that hadn't been as heightened before. I could see the impossibility of other people's circumstances. Fred had been in a terrible position with me. He had loved me – as truly as a person could – and because of that, he'd been incapable of telling me no. He'd have given me his every penny, I realised, if I would have given him real love in return. I felt horrible about that. Having so much time without the other tenants was both a good and bad thing. I could process things I hadn't had time to before. I thought about Edie on the road. Where would she go? What would she put up with in order to have a roof over her head? Would she lie down under a bully of a man again? I didn't know the answer to that question. She hadn't reached out to me once since leaving. Maybe that was because she had no access to a phone or even a pen and paper – or maybe she just had no desire to contact me. I was sure she wasn't thinking about me on her travels – except with bitterness, at least. I knew she felt pushed out of her home, but that was the final goal I'd had when I'd first met each one of my tenants. They were all adults, and I knew they couldn't stay with me forever. But I'd hoped there would be a string of tenants that would continue forever – or at least until my last day. I felt differently about that thought now. I was seeing it in a new light, now that I knew how badly things could go wrong. I thought I was in a better position in my former boarding house, barely being able to make ends meet, with minimal responsibility and work to keep my hands busy. I still had work to do, but it wasn't easy work, assigned to me by someone else. I missed not having to make all the major decisions.

That night was the end of everything I'd pegged my dreams on. The reality was that I could never be a saint, no matter what saintly duties I tried to take on. There was always someone waiting to tussle with you, to make your good deeds impossible to carry out. Maybe I had nothing to do with it and I'd just happened to be present at a bad moment. It happens to many unlucky people, but I still knew I'd failed at my most important mission.

I woke up to screaming more blood-curdling than anything I'd ever heard before. At that time, there were no horror movies to watch. We weren't accustomed to it, even in fiction. It was a horrible sound. The female in distress was on the top floor, and I knew I should try to reach her, whatever the outcome. I jumped out of bed before my courage left me and raced up the stairs. I burst in without knocking. Whatever was happening needed fast intervention. I could feel the adrenalin coursing through me. It suppressed the fear I should have felt. The scene was worse than I'd imagined. I'd known it was something serious, but it was more graphic than I'd been prepared for. There was a woman, lying bleeding on the bed. She was completely naked and tied up. Both Jeff and Siobhan were torturing her. I turned and fled to get to the phone. Jeff chased after me. His feet pounded as heavy as fallen steel. I managed to dial the number and it connected. Then I dropped the phone and fought him off. He was hitting and scratching me like a frenzied cat. I clawed my way out of his grasp and kicked him off me. I yelled the address into the phone receiver. I could hear a lady's tone on the other end, but I couldn't make out what she was saying. I just hoped she'd caught all that I'd said. I shouted the information I could think of that she might need to know while Jeff tried to clamp his hand over my mouth. I tried to bite him and spat at him to buy myself time, but he was forceful. I knew as soon as he ended the call that grave injury awaited me. I wasn't sure if he would kill me, but I'd seen the type of depravity he was capable of, and it was evil. I wanted to return upstairs to the lady on the bed, but I knew he'd never let me near her. Siobhan was still with her, and I knew that didn't mean she was safe. If anything, she'd subject her to more now that she had her alone.

I hated that I was in that house. It was a house of horrors. I sobbed hysterically while Jeff kicked and beat me. He didn't relent for a second. I could feel all the hatred he had stored inside him with every blow. I didn't know what had filled him with such rage, but it was undeniable. I played dead just so he'd leave me alone. He must have thought it was pointless to waste another second on me because he drew back and then I heard him pounding up the stairs. I waited and every second felt like it had been converted into hours.

Finally, as I gave way to despair, emergency services arrived. They didn't need to ask me what was going on; they just ascended the stairs to those two people I'd never see again, whose faces were forever etched on my brain. I could hear even more commotion than before. I wanted to join them and give my statement, but I couldn't get to my feet. I felt defeated. The programme I had started with a healthy vision at the centre of it had become something that bled unstoppably. I knew the end had arrived then. Whatever my designs might have been for that house, they had been undone by the events of that day. Removing that couple from the building wouldn't be enough to correct it. I knew that if I brought in a new person, it would invite more trouble. I might have got lucky with a couple of people, but statistically, it felt like it was destined to fail. I couldn't stop crying then. My sobs were silent, but they were hearty too.

The police came first, quickly followed by paramedics. The lady was removed on a stretcher and the other two characters were removed handcuffed. I was so relieved to see them leaving, knowing that they'd never return. But it was sad it had taken that to get rid of them. I knew I'd never shake the images from my mind; they'd forever be lodged in my memory and Edie was gone too. I couldn't ever persuade her to come back, even if I'd known her whereabouts.

The paramedics attended to me too. But I didn't want them to. It felt like I'd earned my injuries. It was my fault – that I'd been so naïve that I'd thought it was possible to save all the people wandering the streets. Maybe they'd chosen to have an uncertain address because it suited their temperaments. Maybe they liked the thrill of being faced with trouble on a daily basis. It was a special area of society that I didn't know enough about. I might have learnt pieces of it, but I didn't want to know the full extent of the evil that existed there.

Chapter Sixteen

I was hospitalised for a week after that. I didn't have internal injuries, but I was badly beaten and bruised. I hadn't even realised how bad it was. I'd been distracted by what was happening around me. I knew I'd been the lucky one in that situation. The poor woman that was attacked by them passed away shortly after. I'd hoped her injuries weren't life-threatening, but they must have been more forceful than I'd even realised. Part of me always wished I'd put myself between them instead of running for the phone, but I knew that if I had, there would have just been two funerals instead of one.

As soon as I was discharged from hospital, I arranged for the house to be sold. I planned to take the money from its sale and use it to fund my room in a boarding house. That was where I had belonged from the start. I was a simple being. There was no point in trying to be complex. I didn't think the place would sell easily. It was grand-looking, but so much had happened there, it felt like it clung to the walls. I couldn't stay there while I waited for it to sell. The atmosphere was contaminated by what had occurred there.

I never heard anything else about Jeff or Siobhan. I assumed they had both been imprisoned for a good portion of their lives, if not the entirety of them. It was better for everyone like that. I thought of the streets and the fact they were safer then. That was the only saving grace in what I'd done. I'd removed two people from the street that could have done major damage to other people. When I thought about Jeff's fragility on our first meeting, it struck me just how talented he'd been at lying. He'd inspired such pity in me, but he'd been a predator all along. I knew that he couldn't have solely been influenced by Siobhan. You couldn't be convinced to do something that evil unless it already existed inside you on some level. I wanted to put the whole experience behind me and forget it, but it felt like it stalked me. The memory of it kept intruding on my thoughts any time I tried to think of something else. It was tortuous.

I found a new place to live. It was as basic as the place I'd originally lived in as a single worker. I wanted to return to working. I needed to do something to keep my hands and my mind busy, to make it feel like I still had a purpose. I didn't know what I was meant to do with the rest of my days on Earth. Nothing obvious sprang to mind. The plan I'd had that would fill my every waking moment was no longer present and that was hugely disappointing. I wondered what Fred would think of me if he found out. Maybe he'd never known what I was working at. There had been a couple of news articles in the papers about it. But there was no way of knowing if he had read them. I wanted to serve him in some way, but I knew I couldn't show my face there again either. My divorce settlement seemed like a pay-off too. Maybe it was a way of satisfying me, so I'd stay far away from him. He might have had another wife by then – or a girlfriend at least. I could never again impose on him, even if he remained in the home we'd shared. He was better off than I was because he slept with a clear conscience. In the end of the day, that was the only thing in life that mattered – reaching the end of a day and knowing that you'd done the best you possibly could with it. I wondered if he ever had a moment of self-reproach regarding our failed union, but it had never been his fault. I was the one with badness living inside me. I hadn't been able to feel love for him, no matter how much I had worked at it. I hoped he would find someone that could, but I knew I would have been slightly jealous if I'd been replaced, and I didn't know why. Maybe that phase of my life had been the most stable one, even if it had been unfulfilling. I thought about my parents, and I knew that it was better they hadn't lasted long enough to see my current state.

The boarding house smelled bad. It was very damp and cold. But it was home to me. It was what I was used to – what I felt I deserved. Living somewhere more luxurious had never sat right with me. I got a job doing laundry for the locals. It was hard work on my hands, and I ended up with burst blisters from all the scrubbing. They began to close overnight and reopened in the morning when my hands were worked hard again. I didn't care. That kind of discomfort didn't upset me as much as emotional discomfort did. It was satisfying, knowing that I was working myself to the bone and seeing the results of it on my hands. I was praised for the quality of my work. I could work quickly and methodically – without sacrificing anything in quality. The clothes I cleaned were as new as they'd been upon first wear. I knew I was doing what I was supposed to do, even if it didn't feel significant. Maybe it didn't have to be. Plenty of people made their way through life without doing anything others considered to be significant. They were content with that, so why did I feel that I always had to achieve something great? It was egotistical and I knew it. I wanted to allow myself to find contentment in doing the simplest things. It was a calmer mode of existence, but I knew I deserved to be punished too, for my treatment of Fred. I could never rest because of that. It kept me up many nights. Even though my body was tired, I couldn't find the sleep I needed. There were so many disturbances – if not in my conscious mind, then in my dreams. In nearly every dream I had, I was back in Fred's house, repaying his kindness with my service. I had never left him in my sleep. I was still sitting there – a constant companion. That was enough for me then. When I woke up, the shame returned to me. I had allowed him to use so much money for my good and I'd never forgive myself for that, even if he did.

I made a new life for myself. And eventually, despite my misgivings, the house sold to a reliable buyer. They didn't know the history of it, and I decided there was no need to fill them in on it. It would have no personal impact on them. They could make of the house what they wanted. I just hoped they'd never pick up on the bad feel of it. I didn't want to pass that on to another person, especially when they'd been nothing but pleasant to me.

I was only forty years old, but I had the sense that I was running out of time. I might have been at the midpoint of my life median-wise, but I knew I was nearing the end. People just know things like that about themselves. It's like the people with short lifelines that don't expect themselves to last long. A friend of the family always recounts after the funeral how the person noted their short lifeline at an earlier stage, and everyone dismissed it as superstition, but the owner's premonition always came to fruition. I felt like that. I'd never examined mine until I had that thought, but I realised then that it ended suddenly, halfway between my thumb and the point where my hand met my wrist. It felt significant, but I had no one to tell.

I knew the other residents in the new boarding house less than I'd known any in a previous boarding house. I kept to myself and kept my head down. I worked hard for every penny I earned, and I tried to live quietly, so I didn't disturb anyone or cause the least bit of trouble. I wanted to be welcome there for good. Boarding houses always feel like temporary accommodation, but I knew for me they would have more permanence than anywhere else I'd stayed.

I appreciated every day I was given. I thought of them as gifts from above, even though I had dismissed the notion of God. I couldn't sever myself from my Christian roots, however much I might have wanted to cut myself free from them. Nothing remarkable was happening to me – nothing that made good material for a book, but I was carrying on with my existence, in spite of the enormous disappointment I'd felt. I hoped that counted for something.

Chapter Seventeen

The end came to me sooner than I'd anticipated. I started to feel very sick. I didn't know what was causing it. I'd always been bountiful with regards to good health, even when other things ailed me. I knew there were sicknesses that passed around more prolifically then, but I'd never considered it a possibility that I could contract one of them. I was bed ridden within days. My work was waiting for me, and I couldn't even elevate my head. I needed my bodily strength, but it was gone. I felt old and helpless. Everything else in the house carried on as normal. I could hear all the sounds of daily living, but I wasn't a part of them anymore. No one seemed to notice that I hadn't left my room. It was better in a way. I knew I'd rather quietly fade away than cause a stir. I was sure I was ill, but I had no idea what was wrong. I didn't have the energy to leave the room and I didn't want to have to call on anyone for help. I had reached a place of acceptance, of the fact that I mightn't get better, and that it mightn't have been the worst thing in the world if I didn't. It didn't feel like there was something exciting up ahead that I'd miss out on if I passed on. I was delirious. I had a bucket in the room that I had to use as a toilet. There was no one to clean it out, so it just remained there, polluting the air of the room. I was too sick to care. I was glued to my bed. The sheets stuck to my back and no matter how many times I peeled them away from the tender skin, they stuck again straight away. It was distressing, but I was so far away in my mind that it spared me some of the discomfort.

I could hear the sounds made by the house, amplified. They hurt my ears and I tried to find peace underneath my pillow, but there was none to be found. Eventually, after a long time had passed, one person came to the door. They said they could smell a stench coming from the room. I tried to call out to them, but my voice came out too weakly. I could see the door handle turning and I warned them to stay away. That was the point at which someone sent for a doctor. I'd never felt so helpless in my life. I couldn't support the weight of my body on my two legs. I had to hold onto something to pull myself up. I managed to hide the bucket out of view, but I knew they would find it anyway. It was demeaning. I hadn't eaten in days, nor did I have the desire to eat. The thought of the blandest foods repulsed me. I knew I was getting skinny. I was as thin as a street urchin, and I knew I probably looked as dirty as one too. I hadn't managed to wash myself once that week, and the sweat had been rolling off me every day, collecting on the sheets, gathering in my pores and running out all over again.

The doctor finally arrived and let himself into the room. There was no lock on the door, and I was grateful for that then. I was so weak, and I kept drifting in and out of consciousness. I still couldn't fathom what was wrong with me, but I knew it must have been serious. The doctor stayed at a distance from me, but he looked me over with all his metal implements. It was dehumanising, resting there while he attended to me. It was a glimpse of the animal world when humans take over and the animals have no say. But I desperately needed his help too.

He told me in gentle tones that I had TB. I'd heard of it before; I'd had an aunt that had died of it. But I didn't know what it meant. Was it a deadly disease, I wondered, or just something that wiped you out until the wonderful release of recovery? The landlady was lurking in the background, and I could see the look of concern on her face. I didn't think she cared about me a bit, so it made me think it really must have been something bad. I could just see her face floating there, like it was moving independently from her body. Nothing felt real. The doctor prescribed some medication, but the look on his face told me there wasn't much he could do. He sternly instructed the landlady to quarantine me. There was no one to look after me, and I wouldn't have wanted them to employ anyone to do it. The way I saw it – I was meant to be helping others then and I had failed at that. Instead, I was lying, like an invalid, awaiting the call of death's doorbell. The doctor closed the door softly behind him. Thankfully, he'd told the landlady to take away my toilet and to bring a clean one to the door. I had to get my way to the door to collect it, but I had all the hours of the day to do it. It made me feel pathetic – that I had to rely on a woman I barely knew to enable me to carry out the most basic of human functions.

I watched the walls of my rooms, seeming to swell and then curve, undulating with fever. I was so hot that I couldn't stop shivering. Clamminess had become profuse sweating and I felt like I couldn't stay awake for longer than a few minutes at a time. Nightmares kept pulling me back, like currents pulling me underwater, time and again.

After an entire morning of encouraging myself out of the bed, I managed to collect the clean basin and return to the bed. I caught a glimpse of myself in the mirror. I was like a whispered story of someone that used to exist. My face was sunken in, and I was so off-colour I couldn't even find a shade to name it. On top of that, I had developed a cough and my chest was so tight I couldn't take a single satisfying breath. I became aware, in my sleep state, of movement inside the room. I didn't know who it was or why they were there. Anything was possible in that house. I could have been robbed while I slept, but I knew they'd be disappointed with what they found. I assumed my job was long gone. I hadn't attended work in weeks, and I hadn't been able to explain why to my employer. She was a jolly lady, but you didn't want to get on her bad side either. I knew she'd be the type that thinks you should trail yourself to work on you two hands if your legs ceased to work.

There were flies rattling in the window, incessantly, and I couldn't stop them. It was maddening to listen to, but there was nothing I could do about it. It felt like they were tormenting me on purpose. But maybe they just felt how I did: that they were trapped inside bodies that wouldn't function how they needed them to, that they were trapped behind glass with no hope of ever breaking through it. I had some empathy for them then. But I knew that if I'd been more vivacious, I would have given them an instant thwack with the nearest newspaper. They were still dirty and irritating. I didn't know what their purpose was. I knew a lot of people could have said the same thing of me, but I tried to console myself with the few memories I had of the times I'd helped others, or tried to, at least. That was all that remained in my mind at the end; it was my only consolation for a life disappointingly led.

I rapidly got worse and worse. I was getting the montage in my mind of all the significant memories of my life. It wasn't like a film being wrapped up with a tidy ending. I wanted to tie off all the loose ends that remained, but there was no resolution to so much of what had happened. I got so sick that I couldn't get out of bed for any reason. Only then, was a nurse called in to care for me. She was wearing protective gear and I knew just how infectious I was and why I had been alone for so long. Each breath I took was laborious. I felt so guilty for having taken it for granted up until that point: clear breathing. It was a luxury I no longer enjoyed.

Finally, I passed away in my sleep. It was better that way. I would rather have moved on and joined my parents, I decided, than remained in that bed getting sicker than I could ever have imagined feeling. I didn't expect to automatically be reunited with my parents. I might have tried the best I could to lead a decent life, but I didn't know if I'd ever be forgiven for turning away from my faith. I knew if there was one thing I would be eternally punished for – that would be it.

Chapter Eighteen

I saw the light that everyone refers to – but it wasn't bright like the famed kind. I wondered if mine was more toned down because heaven didn't await me. It felt like I was just existing in that lit passageway, waiting forever for something to happen. It was like waiting for death, only with less certainty. At least with illness, I knew what the physical steps were. With the spiritual realm, it wasn't anything as clearly defined as that. I waited for someone to tell me what to do. It was strange, sitting there, looking into emptiness. It made me realise that life was different. There had always been someone nearby to ask for directions. I didn't feel afraid though; I felt a strange sense of calm. It was the only time I'd ever felt like I had nothing to do, or nothing I could be doing. I didn't know what was coming next, so my mind couldn't even explore the possible options.

Eventually, I was led by something I couldn't see. I just knew it was there – like you can feel the wind breathing on you without ever seeing it. I followed it down a long, dark corridor. It spoke to me, but not in a language. It was like we communicated without words. I had so much I wanted to ask it. I was afraid of being left behind again. The route we'd taken wasn't welcoming and I was getting frightened that I was about to enter the pits of hell. I could think of so many reasons why I might have to do that. I would have been beyond surprised if I'd immediately been reunited with my parents in paradise. There was no question in my mind that they'd be there. They had followed their faith for the entirety of their lives. I regretted the fact that I hadn't done the same. I'd had ample opportunity for it, but it was too late. I was always waiting for the belief in it to strike me, like a bolt of lightning - an awakening. It had never come, but I hadn't spent much time looking for it either. I knew I'd prioritised things that weren't as important over that. But when I'd been on Earth, the spiritual world was irrelevant to me. It was too easy to get distracted by the issues at hand. It was like trying to pay attention to a quiet whisper in a loud room. It was easier to just submit to the power of the louder sound.

The corridor we walked down was unattractive. There was nothing that stimulated the senses like a tunnel in the physical world. But there was an air of dampness and depression to it. It felt like we were travelling closer and closer towards unhappiness, and I didn't want to go. But I had to follow my guide. I knew she was female, and she must have been important in a way. She knew exactly where we were going, but she didn't give me any indication of what it might look like. I was miserably cold, and my teeth were chattering. It was strange because I knew I didn't have the enamel ones I'd had prior to my demise. But the discomfort was still there, just the same. I didn't need them to suffer. I couldn't remember what my name was then. I knew I'd had an identifying title on the Earth, but I'd forgotten it. I knew I didn't need to know it anymore. That fact made me sad, but when I plumbed the depths of my memory, it was long gone. It was like the "I" as an individual no longer mattered, or maybe I'd just been so sinful in life that I was being wiped out as punishment for it. The place had a smell of death and decay. The lower we travelled, the worse it got. All the senses merged to make one, and it was overwhelmingly strong. I was led for what felt like miles. The anticipation seemed worse than whatever could await me at the end. But I couldn't have dreamt up what my punishment would be either.

Chapter Nineteen

Eventually, I walked into a cobwebbed room. When I moved through the webs, they stuck to me like goose grass. I shook them off, but it was useless because they just stuck to me again with each new step. The being that led me there told me she was leaving. I wanted to reach out and grab onto her. I didn't want to be alone again. The loneliest feeling I'd ever experienced had been waiting in that holding room for someone to come and meet me, not knowing if anyone ever would. I didn't want that to happen again, but when I did reach out to her, my hand moved through her. She was just a mirage and so was I, it seemed. I couldn't grasp anything around me. It made it hard to tell whether my surroundings weren't real or whether I wasn't. I knew I was still thinking, but that was all I had left.

I stood alone in the room, waiting in the cobwebs. They tickled me all over, in a way that felt entirely unpleasant. I knew there was something unimaginable coming. It was like a nightmare I was forever trapped in. I could remember dying, but I couldn't remember much else. I was struggling to recall what I had spent my life doing. I knew it was the key to everything. I'd probably be forced to endure a harsh consequence served to me by God, if I was even allowed in His presence for long enough to have it shared with me. I waited to hear the screams of eternal torment that I had imagined. I didn't know where I was, but I supposed it was somewhere like limbo. Then, another presence appeared before me. It looked beautiful, but not like an angel I'd seen in illustrations. I supposed that was all just a human interpretation of the afterlife. Then I wondered where those pictures had come from and why they were presented that way. People always need to be given a clear picture of everything to make sense of it in their heads, but maybe the over-simplification of it was what had made me unable to believe in it. The story of the Bible was too perfect to seem real to me. There might have been stories of woe in it and examples of human failure, but they were presented in such a simple way, it had made the book unrelatable to me.

I thought about Fred the most then. He had probably got to keep his life because of how well he had lived it. He was a good person and the rewards for that had been awarded to him. I didn't begrudge him that at all. It just felt like justice was finally being served, but that didn't make it easy to face. I was still human and afraid for myself. Fear didn't go away just because something seemed fair to you. Self-preservation was a strong instinct.

A presence appeared before me and led me silently towards my fate. The place was horror inspiring. It was filled with such thick webs the ones that came before seemed like mere wisps. I couldn't move through them. They had substance even though nothing else did. There was something loud moving towards me. It sounded like a giant's approach. I had no idea what it could be and that made it worse. I couldn't hear myself thinking over each surly stomp it made. I tried to crouch down, but I couldn't disentangle myself from the webs.

"You have to work your way out of your punishment," said the presence. It didn't have any of the distinctive features of a voice. It just sounded powerful without having a particular tone.

"What do you mean?" I croaked.

My voice had disappeared. I didn't know if it had heard me, but the response told me it had.

"I can't give you clear instructions. You just need to examine your conscience for the answers."

"Am I in hell?"

"Hell doesn't exist – apart from our own personal hells we bring upon ourselves."

The voice was growing in volume, but I still couldn't work out exactly what it belonged to.

"I have to leave you now," it continued, "But if you look at your heart, you'll know why you're here and how to get out."

"Is God punishing me?"

"God?"

"Yes, for turning away from my faith."

"No, God isn't real," said the voice, "At least not in the way so many people think."

"What is it?"

"The great juror. You're here for your judgement, but there is no hell, unless you choose it through your own insensitivity."

I couldn't comprehend what it meant. If there wasn't a Christian God, then I wondered, where were my parents? In a way, it had been a comfort to me, thinking that He existed and that my parents might be happy in heaven, even if I was excluded from it. I still loved them unconditionally and I wanted them to be spared whatever I might suffer.

The voice left my side, and I was alone with the terrifying pounding building and building until it was louder than any sound I'd ever heard in life. Being right on the runway when a plane took off didn't even equal it; nothing could. I was experiencing a level of fear I hadn't known possible. I knew I'd felt it in my life, but I couldn't remember my own actions, or the direct cause of my fear. Maybe that was part of my punishment. I had to work out what I'd done, but it wouldn't return to me easily. I'd have to speak to my conscience and wait patiently enough to hear its answer.

Eventually, the producer of the sound was revealed to me. A huge spider appeared before me. It was so many times bigger than me that it was hard to see the full picture of it. But I saw its hair-coated legs and I knew what it was without having to question it. It was staring straight at me, like it was contemplating whether I'd make a good lunch. I cowered as much as I could with my limbs held fast. I knew it could read my fear. There was a distant memory of something related to spiders, but it was so vague I couldn't remember what it was. The spider watched me for a painfully long time. I was waiting for it to strike. I wanted it to be done with it, however it may hurt me. I was frozen and the fear was seeping into every cell of my body in such large doses I couldn't bear it. I vomited then and tried to direct it away from the predator. I didn't want to do anything to draw further attention to myself. Even though it was staring straight at me, some naïve hopefulness in me told me that maybe it didn't see me. I hoped it was looking through me, like daydreamers look through friends they pass in the street. I couldn't allow myself to breathe. If I was, it was inaudible. I was still familiarising myself with my current form. Maybe breathing wasn't required then, but it felt like I was still doing it. It was a confusing state of affairs - on top of all the terror. I felt like I could have died from fear, had I not already been dead.

The spider finally pounced on me. It was so strong I barely knew what was happening to me. It knocked me off my feet and my head spun. I knew I probably had a concussion, or something more serious. I was stunned, but I was still awake. It wrapped me in its satin thread, tighter and tighter until I could see nothing. I thought it was going to eat me whole, but the bite never came. I couldn't see a thing. I just saw white in front of my eyes, like I was inside a body bag. I knew it was probably better to be spared the view. I couldn't keep my eyes open any longer; the tension of the web was too tight, and it was blinding me. I surrendered to whatever was to come.

Chapter Twenty

The binding was horribly tight, but it didn't break. It seemed that the spider planned to keep me there for a late-night snack. I wondered how many other unfortunate entrapments had taken place in that web. I couldn't see the others and they couldn't see me. Maybe it was better that we couldn't see the fear in each other's eyes. But it was scarier imagining that there was no one else there – that it was my own personal hell and no one else would ever join me.

I could hear the spider approaching and then receding into the background. I didn't know why it kept doing that, but it was terror-inducing. I knew it was sent to torment me, but I didn't understand what the aim of it was. I racked my brains, but I couldn't find one solitary memory that seemed relevant to the predicament I found myself in. My mind was frozen with the shock of everything too, and I wasn't even clear on how it was possible I still had conscious thoughts. I thought those were left behind with my physical body, but I supposed the spirit outlived the body. I stayed there, suspended in the air, feeling utterly hopeless. I hoped someone might come to my aid, but they wouldn't until I figured out whatever lesson I was meant to learn. The spider came and left, came and left, and however many times it approached me, the fear never subsided. I never fell into a false sense of security when silence returned. I made a feeble attempt at tearing the web away from myself, but it was fruitless.

I wished I could return to my life. I was saddened by the loss of it – by the fact that I'd never be able to correct what had been done on Earth. I didn't know if the voices that instructed me would ever return, but I hoped they would. I needed to be rescued; there was no way I could extricate myself from the thick web that surrounded me. It was stuck to me like superglue sticks to skin. I'd thought that silk spun by spiders was a delicate material, but I suppose it depended on the size ratio. I thought of the webs I had swept away in my lifetime. They'd always been a nuisance, dirtying corners, and ceilings of rooms, making my books less readable, preventing me from reaching into small spaces in the dark. I'd torn many a masterpiece apart without a second thought. But so had every other human on Earth, I thought. I knew the amount of work that went in to making it, but I'd never stopped to consider that. It was like a sculpture made by a talented artist; it was much more than just a net to catch dinner with. I felt a twinge of sympathy for the plight of the spider. They'd been trampled over in so many ways – figuratively and in their bodily form too.

I felt like the binding was loosening a little, but I knew that could have been my mind playing tricks on me. I hadn't budged an inch since I was laid to rest there. So, I knew that if I was ever freed, it would have to be by someone else's hands.

In some ways, being bound there was a mercy; I couldn't see what unfolded before me. I could sense the spider's feelings and it made me realise for the first time that it had them. It wasn't so unlike me, but the roles had been reversed. It felt like that was the beginning of a realisation, but I was still unsure of what it was. I was slowly unwrapped, like a mummy revealed beneath bandages. I knew I was moving on to another place, but I dreaded to think where it was.

I couldn't feel my body when it was unwound. It was numb from being held so tightly. I stood in front of the spider, looking at it, face to face. It was godlike in comparison to me. I felt so insignificant standing there. It scuttled away, to the top of its web and turned its back on me. I took the opportunity to run. I knew it was granting me that chance too. But I didn't know what might come next. I didn't know where I was going. I was completely disorientated, and it wasn't comforting leaving one place of captivity to go in search of another.

Chapter Twenty-One

I put one wobbly foot in front of the other. It was either that or turn back and return to the web for good. I ended up in another room. When I was there, I could hear cries of torment and it pained me to hear them. I didn't know what they were suffering from, but I knew it must have been personally tailored to their fears. I was closed in a room that was all glass. Every wall was made of windows and the air was suffocating. I climbed the glass and kept sliding back down it. I knew I could only get so high, but logic didn't matter to me. I just knew I had to try to get out. I butted my head against the glass, hoping it might shatter and free me. I didn't care if I got cut. In that place, maybe I couldn't sustain physical injuries anyway. I had somehow walked away from the enormous spider unscathed. I knew it was all a mental lesson, but it felt real in every sense of the word.

I didn't know what was coming next, but I knew in my bones that it was something bad. I had to escape before my fate fell upon me. I was the only person in the room. I almost wished I had the company of others. Maybe if we couldn't escape, we could have at least panicked together. It would have been like a strange kind of bonding experience – like being held hostage creates families out of complete strangers.

I flailed myself against the glass. It made loud squeaky noises and I felt like it was almost laughing at me. What was ordinarily an inanimate object, suddenly became something with the power of a person. I could hear a noise in the background. I was petrified, but I was focussed on my mission too – to hurry up and escape. I knew my time was limited. I heard the noise getting closer. It was as deafening as a million decibels. I grimaced at it, but I didn't attempt to cover my ears; my hands were too occupied with the pointless task of climbing the window. There was no frame to it – it was just glass on all four sides – seemingly standing up on its own, but perfectly solid. I threw myself against it, praying it would break, but I knew it wasn't going to shatter. It was like trying to shatter bulletproof glass. It had been designed for punishments like mine. Or maybe it had come into creation specifically for me. There was no way of knowing how many rooms there were, like cells of suffering, created for however many people needed them. It sounded to me like a last stab at salvation, but I didn't know what that meant anymore. If my parents' god wasn't real, what was in His place? I thought he must have been punitive to have set up a system like that. It almost would have been kinder to condemn everyone. I pictured a grand judge, sitting invisibly on the other side of the glass, delighting in the lessons being delivered. But they didn't have easy exits and you had to work them all out for yourself to stand a chance at survival – whatever survival stood for in the spiritual world.

A deep voice came. It was so loud I couldn't hear what it was saying. Then I noticed the owner of it. It was a human, but it was like a giant. He was carrying something, rolled up in his hand, but I didn't know what it was. Seeing everything out of proportion made it hard to identify anything – even familiar objects. As he got closer and closer, I recognised the irritation on his face. He was complaining about something; I knew it from his tone. His speech was so amplified that it was like trying to hear the complaint of wind as you walked through a wind tunnel. It was something so big that it became general rather than specific. I tried to flee, but the thing in its hand was coming down upon me hard. I jumped out of the way, just missing it. Then, I could remember what the object was – it was a rolled-up newspaper. I remembered using them myself when I needed to. I wanted to beg and plead for my life. It was a cruel way to die - having the life squashed out of you, just because someone decided to. I knew I was probably making a noise against the glass that was irritating, but it was just a natural response. I didn't want to annoy the man. I didn't want to draw any attention to myself. He probably thought I was doing it intentionally – like a wasp that comes back harder every time you bat it away. I was just a wasp to him, even if I was a much more complex organism.

I kept fleeing, but my energy was getting low, and he was determined to get me. There was no corner in which to hide. I was exposed on every inch of glass. I couldn't even retaliate. You can't fight off something thousands of times the size of you. I realised then that I'd known nothing of real fear in my lifetime. I might have had my trials but nothing to that extent. I must have been flattened right after I had that thought because I wasn't aware of anything for a long time after it. When I awoke, I was very surprised. I'd thought it was all over – for good. Dying after death felt as final as you could get. But I hadn't – I'd been spared.

It took me a while to properly come around. When I did, I realised I was in a different room again. This time, I was one of a thousand larvae. It was horrible when I realised the sum of my existence. I was just one forgotten piece of an enormous family. We were all crawling around together, but none of us knew where we were going. It was survival of the fittest within my own family. I knew we were related, but it wasn't like having brothers and sisters. I didn't know any of their names, and it wasn't worth asking. None of us were named anyway. I knew if I happened to die, no one would notice. It was up to me to make sure I didn't. I wasn't even sure that living was the better option in that life. I'd heard of the concept of reincarnation, but that was just ridiculous. I felt like I'd been reduced to nothing. I stayed there for a long time, just squirming around aimlessly. I wasn't making the slightest bit of progress. It didn't feel like my progress made any difference in that life. Even if I made it out of the early stages, where would I end up? I didn't have wonderful prospects – none of us had, and I couldn't find any consolation for that in my conscious mind. I knew I was lucky to still have human thoughts inside my head. I doubted the others had that. They acted on instinct alone. They couldn't think things through or come up with ideas; they were just getting by on their desire to avoid death.

It felt like I stayed in that state for much longer than was biologically possible. When the moment came, I was delighted to leave. I knew I wasn't finished. It didn't feel like I'd had an epiphany yet. But I was so tired. It was like sleep deprivation to a human body. I was striving to remember everything that I'd done, but it was so hazy. I knew there was so much of it, it was like trying to sort through years of disorganised papers, looking for one specific page. But I didn't have time to stop and think. I was being driven forwards at a speed I could barely keep up with.

I felt sorry for the flies – the little forgotten maggots that didn't have a chance at life. They were fighting so hard to survive, but no one noticed it. I could feel my awareness expanding, but I still didn't know the definitive answer.

I was reborn, it seemed, in a body with eight legs. I knew I was a spider, and I had no idea why. Was it a punishment or a reward? The people with the answers were nowhere to be seen anymore. I didn't know why I was on the other side of the equation then. I'd been allowed to become predator rather than prey. I was in the process of spinning a web. It was much harder work than I'd ever realised. I'd thought spiders created webs solely to disturb the environments around them – like an act of possessiveness. But it was clear to me then, just how much work they put into what they created. I knew how to do mine, but that didn't make it effortless. I had to think about the pattern and the dimensions and how to strengthen it. Apart from feeling an instinctive need to finish my work, I knew my food supply depended on it too. I was starving and the thought of flies for dinner sounded appetising. I knew I needed a good web. Having been a spider for only a matter of moments, I didn't know the best techniques to lure them to my web yet.

I was listening with all my senses for the approach of my dinner. It was like fishing. I'd only done it once as a child, but when I'd been sitting there, I'd noticed so many fishermen, patiently awaiting their dinner. They'd been ultra-focussed on what they were doing, and I hadn't even seen them look away from their line once. But they were also able to man the fishing rod without seeming to grip it too tightly. Every time I heard a buzz, I stood closer. It was like a feeding call that kept teasing me when there were no results. I was starting to think I was destined to starve as a spider. it wasn't an easy existence; I was quickly learning that. Finally, after hours of fruitless waiting, a fly landed in my net. I had to act quickly. I couldn't afford to have it come unglued. It was panicking. I'd never thought the buzzing meant anything before, until I heard it up close. It sounded even worse on that level. The fly was bargaining, begging me to free it. It still had a chance of completing its day, but it all depended on me.

I decided to ignore the call of my belly. It would only satisfy me in the short term. I couldn't kill the fly, now that we were on the same level. Seeing him up close and hearing his pleas made me feel terrible. He was a person then - not just an animated source of irritation. It was mildly annoying that my web needed repaired, but I knew then that I'd starve as a spider because I couldn't go through with capturing my food. I unwound the threads around him, apologetically. He was still in despair, sharing his every fearful thought with me. It was strange to know that the buzzing that had plagued me had really meant something. Maybe my words had been nothing but noise to the flies too. I still didn't know how the lesson was relevant to the life I'd lived. I thought that perhaps it was a metaphor for something bigger. I didn't realise then that the small things counted as much as the big things. The hierarchy I placed them in wasn't real. I'd been so worried about being judged for the biggest things that I'd never stopped to consider the smallest ones.

Chapter Twenty-Two

I released the fly. It didn't show me any gratitude and I didn't blame it. It flew across the room, completely dizzy and disoriented. I didn't know what the rest of its day or life would be like thereafter; I'd done my bit for it. I was sure there was a multitude of spiders awaiting him on his journey home, but at least I hadn't yielded to my inbuilt instincts. I didn't want to be a spider anymore. It was causing me such discomfort, regarding my own long, black legs. I'd always been afraid of spiders, and now that I was one, that hadn't changed. I couldn't see my reflection unless I went looking for it, but my legs were visible to me. Another fly landed in my net. Part of me wondered why if I'd already passed the test. So, I resisted the temptation to eat it and freed that one too. I could tell they were greatly affected by their encounter with me, but they were also surprised when I released them. I supposed it was something that didn't happen often in spider society.

As soon as I freed the second fly, my position changed again. I came around and I was in another small body, but this time it was brown and six-legged. I was in a long line and my feet were marching along without me having to manoeuvre them. There were hundreds of other creatures just like me and we were carrying something over our heads. I could feel the weight of it, but I didn't seem to consciously consider it either. I just plodded on. It was teamwork at its best. I thought that perhaps it was a lesson in teamwork that I had missed out on in life. But I could have applied that to so many situations that it was impossible to narrow it down. We walked for what felt like hours, following the line of the wall. I wondered if we were ever going to eat. It was tiring work, and no one suggested stopping or setting down our load. We just kept going, following the leader of the line, assuming he or she knew exactly where they were going and why we had to wait. My legs felt like they were buckling beneath me, but I had to keep going for the common good.

Everyone was panting but no one was complaining. They were harder workers than I'd met in human form. I could see how valuable their enterprise was. They were united in delivering their food to the chosen destination. Just as I was feeling proud to be part of it, there came a disruption. One of the ants in front of me began to scream. There was something large, flat and plastic coming down on our heads. It just missed us, and everyone shrieked. It wasn't over though; the object was relentless in its pursuit of us. It was determined to crush one, if not all of us. I couldn't even see where it was coming from, but I heard shouting. It was a loud voice, but it was so loud that I couldn't make out what it was saying. I knew whatever was producing it was angry. The plastic came down on us again and again, and a couple of ants dropped to the ground. I knew we wouldn't go anywhere without them, so we were stuck were we were. I just hoped whoever was using the plastic spade would give up. A couple of us were injured, but overall, it didn't have the best aim. I knew we were miniscule in comparison to it though. One well-aimed hit would have been enough to finish us all off. It would have been kinder in a way, than terrifying us with so many missed strikes. I noticed that one ant had collapsed behind me. I hadn't had time to get to know him well, but he'd seemed like a cheery fellow. I prodded at him, but he didn't produce the slightest reflex. I asked the other ants what was going on and they looked at me in the same way parents look at their children when they break a family death to them. I was one of the young learners, and I was meeting our worst-case scenario on day one. I knew I'd never survive as an ant, or as any other insect, and I felt a sudden respect for all living creatures – even the ones that I'd thought nothing of in my lifetime. I wanted to look after them. But I knew that I couldn't save them. The thing coming down on us was a fly swatter, and a heavy boot followed. It took out half our army of ants. I was one of the luckier ones. We managed to flee, but we had to leave our food behind us. We'd worked so hard to carry it to that point and we'd have to start over again, but we didn't have the time to be discouraged. We were just happy to leave with our lives. The remaining ants conversed with each other, but it was all work-related. They were coming up with a new strategy to get some days-old bread. I was famished, but we all were, and I just tried to ignore the hollowness of my stomach. We were all in the exact same position. I remembered then how easily I had come upon food. I mightn't have always eaten the fanciest foods, but there had always been food in abundance. I thought of the soups we shared in the boarding house and the lengths I would have gone to, to get a taste of it then. We lay low for the rest of the day then. It was too risky to go back out. I knew the fly swatter would be waiting for the ones that it had missed. The person wielding it obviously had a lot of contempt for insects. Maybe they wouldn't sleep that night, knowing that we were in the same room.

We waited for hours and kept busy rearranging our home. It was a little hill that we'd created just outside. We carried dirt up and down on our backs. My back ached worse than it ever had, but we kept going. There was an unspoken agreement between the ants that we weren't allowed to stop moving. We had to be busy all the time, even if our desired task was placed on hold. Once it got dark, we got in line again and agreed to set off in search of food. It took us hours to travel to the kitchen and we were all weak from lack of sustenance. My legs were bowed, and I could see the others were feeling the same. But we kept upbeat and sang a song together, to keep our spirits up. We stayed as close to the skirting boards as possible. There were some gaps underneath them that we were small enough to fit under, should the need present itself. We still carried on at a steady speed. Rushing would tire us out and we'd never make it, our leader said. There was one ant at the head of the queue that seemed to be in charge. I wondered who had appointed him or if it was just a birth right of the ants. He was obviously born to do it and I had a lot of respect for him. He kept us as safe as he could, but the danger was unavoidable. The people with the swatters and the huge shoe soles were so big we couldn't see them until the danger was already upon us. That second walk was the time when I got the biggest shock. I thought the man was back. I could hear stomps that sounded like giants' footsteps, and to us they were. We froze and stayed as close to the wall as we could. There was no opening at that point and the master ant commanded us to stand still. I was trembling and I was over-thinking. I wished I had the brain power of a normal insect. It was worse being able to think about all the possible scenarios that could come to us. I wanted to be in the moment, only able to think of survival in the simplest terms.

We waited, hoping the danger would pass. Sometimes we weren't spotted, I'd been told. It all depended on the eyesight and the personality of our attacker. Some people were gentle with insects, and they didn't mind our presence. Some of the ones with the higher pitched voices even thought we were cute. I knew they were talking about children. But there were also some with a sadistic streak. There were stories of terrible things that had happened in the ant community. Some people killed them for the pure pleasure of it, or out of curiosity. We waited and then I recognised the enormous shoe that was coming. I'd worn it myself. I knew as soon as I saw it that we had fallen under my own feet, and I knew our fate with certainty then. I never would have spared an insect in my life. Even if one hadn't been directly annoying me, I had never liked them. I didn't even like them to circle the periphery. I could remember my own feelings of repulsion then. Insects had been a constant in my life – a thing I had never grown to like. No matter where I was stationed and what circumstances I lived with, I had never liked them. My hatred of insects had probably been more constant than my love of anything else. I was seeing the error of my ways, and the extent of my cruelty. I'd probably snuffed out thousands of lives in my lifetime without giving it a second thought.

I saw a flash of hair and I knew the person wearing my shoes was me. It was horrifying, knowing that I was going to squash myself and knowing the thought-process behind it. There was no way out of it. Even if I'd hidden, that person would keep looking for me until they'd disposed of me. It was unfailing – the callousness I showed towards the smallest of creatures.

A swarm of flies suddenly came into the room. They were much noisier than us. I knew her attention had been rerouted. Hopefully by the time it returned to us, we would have had a chance to make our escape. I could see an upcoming gap in the skirting board and the master ant hurried us towards it. We still had to stay in an orderly line, but we picked up our pace.

We made it under the wall. It didn't lead anywhere, but we were safe there. We still hadn't eaten anything, and I knew we were all feeling weak. There wasn't one complaint from my fellow ants. They just kept going, like little soldiers marching through war. I could hear the voice of the human I knew was me. I couldn't bear to tell the other ants. They wouldn't have understood me anyway. I knew it made no sense. Their existence was different to them than it was to me. I knew it served me as part of a lesson, but to them, they were just carrying out their usual duties.

It's funny how one person's story can be irrelevant to someone else in the exact same set of circumstances.

We waited there interminably. I must have finally fallen asleep. When I woke up, I was no longer in an ant's body, and I was no longer sequestered under the skirting board. I felt like I was back in human form – or whatever it was called in that strange realm. I was sitting in an empty room, with nothing to do and no one to talk to. I just waited and waited, hoping someone would show up, but they didn't. That was almost more frightening than having something unpleasant occurring, because at least then, I was active. I had choices about how I responded to the predicament I found myself in. Inactivity was worse. I didn't know what was coming and I only had my thoughts for company. They weren't particularly positive after all that had taken place. I didn't know if I'd learnt my lesson or not – in the eyes of the higher power. I still hadn't met it. I wondered what it wanted from me, and how I was supposed to know right and wrong without the direction of a book. It was strange to think that the entire Bible was invalid; it was just an extended fairy tale. Maybe it held elements of truth and useful fables, but I knew overall, it wasn't what I thought it had been. Even after my childhood had passed by, I'd still believed in its teachings on some level. I mightn't have chosen to follow them, but I thought it was the ultimate truth. I just wasn't made to follow it. I had too much of a rebellious spirit. I'd expected my punishment to be related to that, but everything in my reality had been turned on its head. I wanted to know where my parents were, and how I could reach them, or if I ever would.

I stayed in that room for so long I couldn't have estimated whether it was weeks, months or years. I was still horribly aware of time, even though it didn't exist there. Not having a clock was greatly bothering me. It provided some sort of reassurance, some lasting feeling of control that I then lacked. I mightn't have been able to control the events around me, but I could check my watch, like a constant reference point. It told me that things always passed. Even if you were enduring something nasty, it would come to an end, because all things did. I knew that could be sad too, where death and loss were concerned, but when things had always been moving on. I wished I could accept the fact that I was in stasis. I might have been learning something, but I couldn't see it unfolding in a sequential manner.

I thought about everything that had ever happened to me while I was sitting in that room. With my head clear and my hands empty, I was able to see it all like it was in a photo album before me. I could remember every memory – memorable and forgettable. It was like being tormented by the past, and I hoped it would end once I arrived at whatever realisation the higher power wanted me to experience. I didn't feel like I'd treated anyone particularly well. I thought of Fred in particular, but I also thought of my parents, acquaintances and other living things. I'd always had a soft spot for larger animals, but I couldn't stop thinking about my cruelty towards the insect world. I wondered if that cancelled out my other good deeds. How were they measured? How did you know whether you were doing more right or wrong?

My childhood came back to me with the clarity of a diamond. I saw scenes that I hadn't known I'd forgotten. They'd been filed away somewhere in my mind, never to be revisited in my lifetime. I could remember losing my first tooth. I remembered the blood seeping from my gums and the tooth in the palm of my hand. I could remember my mother reassuring me that it was normal. They'd never mentioned it to me beforehand, and I was struggling to accept that it was. But the calm disposition of my mother made everything immediately better.

I could remember staying up late at night in my bedroom, reading beneath the sheets. I had an oil lamp my mother kept lit at my bedside, to chase the monsters away. She didn't know it had another purpose too. It enabled me to stay up for hours past my official bedtime, absorbing stories of adventure and developing ideas about my own independence. My mother had never found out, and on some level, I'd felt like I was lying to her, however innocent it might have been. I didn't like keeping secrets from people or feeling that the slightest dishonesty existed between us.

I could remember the first time my father was disappointed in me. It had stung like water on newly exposed flesh. He'd never shown any disapproval, until I was in double digits, and then I had invited it in. I'd left the house and hadn't come back until well after dinner time. They didn't know where I'd been, and my mother was in bits. I could still remember her fevered crying. She was intaking breath twice for every exhale. They'd thought I wasn't coming back, and they'd been scared witless. I felt terrible as soon as I saw them. My mother was so upset, but my father was angry. It was the only time I remembered him losing his temper with me, so I remembered it well. It haunted me until adulthood too. It was something I could never completely shake off. It felt like one of those moments that affects you so greatly you're never quite the same again after it. I knew it was nothing compared to the struggles other people have with their parents, but I wondered if my dad fully trusted me after that. I hadn't been doing anything dangerous, but in his eyes, I could have been doing anything under the sun. I sat with that memory for a long time, feeling plagued by guilt. It was unendurable. It seemed like the most significant memory, but I was sure there were others. I flipped through them like a deck of cards, deciding which needed to be pored over the most. They were disorganised, but they were all there.

I didn't dwell on that memory for too much longer. I couldn't change it no matter how much I prodded at it. It was funny that it was a defining moment of my life. It didn't seem like something that should have brought me so much shame. I'd just been seeking my independence as I reached adolescence. I knew that wasn't abnormal, but in those days, your parents' word was law and no one disputed it – unless they wanted to bring disgrace to their family.

I moved on to the next memory. I could remember trying to get my schoolwork done in a timely fashion. We had an ogre of a teacher. But most of them were like that then. It was nothing unusual. I was sure that she was a real tyrant at home if she had a family of her own. We would never know if she did because teachers didn't mix business with their personal lives. I hated every minute we spent with her. It made me appreciate my own parents so much more. She'd stand over us, watching us write, and I couldn't cope with it. Whenever she took the time to do that, my mind would go blank, and I didn't have a hope of answering any of the questions anyway. I had a strong suspicion that I wouldn't go on to do anything academic anyway.

They were coming to me in quick succession – all the moments of my life, with the detail I'd expected in the moment of passing away. It was strange how the smallest and most insignificant details suddenly seemed equally important. I could remember them as if they were happening again and all my senses were engaged in the experience.

My memories seemed to fast forward to a much greater age. I was no longer living at home, and I was working hard and staying in my boarding house. From the outside, the picture I saw of myself filled me with pity. I knew I was working hard and doing whatever I could to lead the best life, but then it was interrupted by my small sins. I hadn't even taken them under my notice at the time. But they were the most important moments when I saw them through that window onto the past. I could see the suffering of every spider, every fly, every moth up close and I could hear their cries. It was heart-wrenching. I saw my own heartlessness and it made me shudder. Then, I could see that all the things I was trying to do were useless. They were cancelled out by what I'd seen as something so small at the time. I hadn't spent a second of my life feeling guilty for it or doubting what I'd just done. I saw scenes of myself working away, working as hard as I possibly could. There were pictures of my hands bleeding from all the clothing repairs and washing I did. I saw myself with my meagre wages at the end of the week, paying them all back into the boarding house. The rooms costed so much for someone on a low wage. I knew it had felt like a struggle, even if I'd felt like there were moments of gratitude for what I had. Even my treatment of my parents didn't seem to have mattered then. I'd harmed living creatures and squashed the lives out of them and there was no way to make up for that. The realisation smacked me in the face. Every other memory was wiped out of my mind and that took precedence. I saw a catalogue of all the times I'd killed a helpless bug and it horrified me. Living as one, even for a short time, had changed my perspective on everything.

I saw the aftermath of what I'd done. I had vacated the room, having thrown the corpse in the bin, or just having left it lying on the windowsill with its legs in the air. The souls of the flies left their bodies and returned to their source. They would get to go to a type of paradise, but it was much more limited than what humans were able to experience. I'd been given a special gift in being human and I hadn't even realised it. It was a privilege that it seemed I had wasted.

My life continued to play out before my eyes. The room I was sitting in was so dark and empty. It was like I was sitting alone in the pictures, and I didn't like it. I just wanted the film to finish, so I didn't have to endure any more scenes of shame, but there seemed to be thousands of them. They were playing in such detail that I got to relive each one, but from an enlightened perspective. It was terrible. I hoped the fact I was feeling such guilt over it would put a stop to them. There was no need to see every single incident. But maybe there was a reason for it that I was too small to comprehend. I listened to the wails of creatures that bled to death, and I felt such shame, that I had caused it. Eventually, I got a slight break from the scenes, to watch the part of my life where I was married to Fred. I saw the concern in my face that I carried around with me for my mother. I could read the strain of it all in my facial expression and I felt sadness for myself. It had been difficult dealing with all of that the first time around, but somehow, knowing how it would all end made it even worse. All the time I spent worrying and trying to correct the situation was nothing but wasted time. My mum would be in the ground months from that point. I could see the effect it was having on Fred. I got glimpses of him that I had missed in my life. It was sad, seeing his brokenness and knowing that I had never tended to it. He'd paid more money than I'd even realised to save my mother, and he had spent countless hours on the phone, pleading with the doctor to save her.

I saw him wilting in the corner of his room, as much as my mother was, but his was a mental death rather than a physical one. I started to cry inconsolably then. I wept so loudly it was like I was a child again, completely lacking in self-consciousness. I didn't care that I was sobbing because no one could hear me. It was a release, but I knew it was only momentary. Soon, the pain would build up again. It was strange, thinking that I had done all I could for my mum and that respecting her wouldn't win me a place in heaven. It didn't matter. I had been undoing all my good deeds in the smallest acts of selfishness and there was no way to remedy that.

I must have been sitting in that room for weeks. It took so long to play the entire story of everything I'd done. Each episode was in real time, and they played without intermission. Finally, when I'd seen every single detail of my misdeeds, it stopped. It was just like the moment when a film ends in the cinema. After all the sound and action and camaraderie, you're left with nothing. There's a moment when everyone sits stunned at the end of a film. I'd only seen one once in my lifetime, as a birthday gift from my dad. It was a major event. People went to the pictures then, but it was still saved for special occasions. And I could remember it so clearly because of that. Sometimes if you do something repeatedly, it creates a blurrier image in your mind that when you've done something just once. I'd never forget that strange kind of silence where everyone readjusted to reality and accepted that the fairy tale was over. It was like they'd been elsewhere and then been dropped back into harsh drudgery. Maybe that wasn't the case for other viewers; but it felt like that – or that they were trying to make sense of the fact that something that captured their attention for hours had come to an end. I expected someone to show up as soon as the film of my life ended, but I was left with nothing but myself for company. I couldn't stop replaying the worst parts of my existence. I was in a state of internal torment and there was nothing to relieve it. I couldn't think of a worse place to be. I would rather have received a clear punishment. Time expanded before me, like an endless desert to a thirsty explorer. There was no end in sight and no glimmer of hope. I must have eventually fallen asleep, but I had vivid dreams that were a continuation of what I'd just seen. The reel of my life was inescapable. I wished I could rewind time and act differently, but I'd already stepped off the cliff edge and reached my so-called resting place.

I knew there was more to come, but I couldn't anticipate what. It had all been so creative – that only a god could have created it. My imagination couldn't have dreamt up what I'd experienced since my passing. In worldly time, I wondered how long had passed, or if it didn't work like that. It was funny how living in a timeless void could make you more aware of time than living by the clock did. I missed having a way to measure it.

I was finally shaken awake. There was nothing gentle about it. I was told to follow the presence that had joined me. I had never met it before and was unclear about who it was. They didn't introduce themselves. It felt like they didn't need to. Their importance emanated from them like light from a bare bulb. I was repelled by the light. It wasn't somewhere I felt like I had the right to be – in the presence of something so holy and pure. I felt like I was dirty then – too dirtied to deserve to be there. It took me by the hand and led me on a long walk. The land we walked through was barren. It was like a sun-scorched wasteland – not somewhere you'd expect to see in the afterlife at all. We walked until my legs ached. I didn't know why I'd held onto physical sensations in that place. Maybe it was because I hadn't entirely passed over yet. I could have been in a kind of limbo – subjected to further testing. I was exhausted, but it didn't matter to me either. I didn't care about how I felt anymore. Feeling good wouldn't have alleviated the terrible guilt I held inside. It was compacted, like a ball of steel in my stomach. I couldn't ignore it if I wanted to. But I knew it was deserved, and that meant I better dealt with it.

The spirit that led me didn't take me by the hand. I thought it didn't want to touch me. If it gave me any sort of human touch, that would have been a kindness I hadn't earned. I followed on its metaphorical coattails, trailing through the land. The weather was dull. It could have been morning, afternoon or night – it was as grey as you can get without becoming black. There wasn't a whisper of wind or a slice of sunlight. I was ready to flee, and I might have if there had been anywhere else to go to. We walked for hours on end without rest. I was more exhausted than I'd ever been from hard work. I could feel my legs seizing up, but I kept putting one in front of the other, without ever questioning how I was doing it. Maybe the power came from whatever god existed. I was running on nothing, and I knew I couldn't do that alone.

Just as I felt like the walk might last forever – a punishment in itself - it came to an end. The spirit opened a door and held it for me so I could walk through first. It became apparent that we were in a courtroom. It looked just like the one in which I'd received the finalisation of my divorce. There was a full jury in house, but they didn't look at me. They were occupied in deep discussion. None of them presented in bodily form but they were made of the most beautiful light I had ever seen. They reduced the most resplendent sunset to a something deserving of a shoulder shrug. Everything was unremarkable in comparison to the purity of that light. It wasn't a particular colour – it could only be defined as beautiful. There were hushed sounds of discussion, but I couldn't make out what they were saying. It was a language I didn't understand – like a holy language I had never learnt. The judge entered the room, and everyone bowed to the ground. I couldn't make out their face, but everyone immediately knew who it was. There was something powerful that came from it – something greater than everything. In the presence of the judge, I felt like nothing but a smouldering ember. I fell to the ground too. Even if I'd resisted that feeling, I couldn't have prevented it. It made my body physically obey.

When the judge spoke, its voice was equally gentle and terrifying. I'd never heard anything like it before. I didn't know why I was there, but I knew there would be a reason for it. Nothing random occurred there. Every single action was orchestrated in such a way that the smallest of details were controlled. I wanted to return to my human life. I felt a tired longing for it that only worsened with each moment's arrival. We were instructed to take our seats. I didn't sit with the jury. They must have been special people – or maybe they'd never been people and they were something like angels. I didn't have the right names for any of what was happening because my only reference point was the Bible and it had all been inaccurate. There might have been some sweeping statements in it that could be applied to morality and spirituality on the whole, but overall, it was a misrepresentation of what came in the afterlife. I thought about my parents again and wondered if their faith had done them any favours. Were they still together? I wondered. I couldn't imagine one happily existing without the other. But if they were in paradise, I hoped that meant they were living together, harmoniously, forever. Maybe if I paid my dues and made up for my sins in life, I would get the chance to join them. I still held out hope for that. I had no choice but to keep going. There was no way to get out of that place like you could from life. It mightn't have been a choice you wanted to make – leaving the world – but at least it was an option. There was nothing like that available to me then.

I was called to the stand. The great presence didn't interact with us one to one – only collectively. There was something very detached about it, but it was also what fed into that feeling of it towering over us. I guessed that was important when you had to make all final decisions on everything, and you had no one's real support. I was in awe of the judge. It was so astonishingly beautiful that I could barely bear to regard it. I didn't dare disturb it or close the gap between us.

I was standing in the pulpit, and I noticed I was shaking with a mixture of respect and terror. It was like the feeling when you quaked in your boots as a child when an angry adult was on the scene. You felt utterly powerless, and you just wanted to vanish out of sight – before they doled out the punishment. Even that childly fear was nothing compared to what I felt in the courtroom.

The place was a strange combination of worldly realism and heavenly glory. The benches were all mahogany, and the rest of the room was filled with faces, like in a regular courtroom. But the strange light only alighted certain faces and everything was enshrouded in a pure light. I knew I didn't deserve to be there, but there I was. I looked down at my clothes, wondering if they had changed to mark the occasion, but I was still wearing the clothing I'd arrived in, and it was threadbare. There was dirt on every inch of it and tears in the fabric. I didn't know what happened when you needed your clothing replaced, or if you were just forced to exist in it until you had to walk around completely exposed. I hadn't ever taken that into consideration before my arrival. I thought that clothing was obsolete in heaven.

The judge addressed me by my name. "Betsy Lewis" - it was like he had given it a whole new meaning. It was the first time I'd heard it since I'd arrived, and finally, it struck me – who I used to be and my old identifier. It filled me with warmth hearing it again. It was like reassurance that I was still a person. I hoped I wouldn't have that entirely removed from me.

I was afraid of what the judge would say. Everyone in the room was staring at me, like they were waiting for the worst. I knew my final judgement was coming and it was petrifying. The warmth from hearing my name quickly changed to what felt like an all-over body chill. I was shaking and I knew everyone could see. I was too scared to feel embarrassed. I wondered how many people had stood in the exact spot I was in and how they had felt. Had my parents stood there? Or was it only reserved for bad people? People that hadn't achieved the only thing that mattered in life: to be a good human being and to bring goodness to the Earth. I hated that I'd wasted my whole lifetime. In eternity, it might have only counted for very little in the grand scheme of things, but I had still made a mess of it.

"Betsy," the judge said. "I hope your lesson has taught you something."

"It has," I said, gravely.

I wasn't sure if it wanted me to give a full summary of all I'd learnt; if the presence was all knowing, there was no need for me to rehash all of it.

"Why do you think you were sent there?" it asked me.

I could assign neither a male nor female sex to the speaker and doing so felt like it would somehow diminish its power.

"To learn where I'd gone wrong and experience it first-hand."

"And what did you do wrong?"

"I was cruel to insects for my whole life."

"It's a long time to be cruel."

"I didn't think it was an uncommon offence."

The presence went silent then, like it was angry with me. I waited for an outburst, or even an on-the-spot condemnation. But it didn't come.

"If killing is common, does that make it ok?" it asked me.

There was nothing comforting about the great judge in that moment. I could feel the power of its wrath and I was afraid it would snuff out my soul in an instant, forever. I knew if that were to happen, I wouldn't know a thing about it, but the thought of not existing was the most terrifying thought of all – even worse than suffering.

I didn't know what sentence they would deliver to me, but I imagined it would be bad. It suddenly felt like the terrible lessons I'd been subjected to were only stage one of my punishment. The jury looked like whatever light they'd held inside them had been extinguished – like they were ready to give bad news. But the presence didn't consult them. It was clear that it was very much in charge. It didn't strike me as being particularly kind, but it was fair. I could feel that energy coming from it, like life from a tree.

"You didn't spare a single insect you encountered in your entire life."

"I didn't know it mattered."

"You didn't know that life mattered?"

"I just didn't stop to consider it. No one taught me it either. I thought I was trying to follow the right path, but I expected to be punished for other things."

"The other things don't matter because this overshadows them all."

"I thought there were larger matters I'd dealt with poorly," I said.

I realised then just how much I was shaking. I was trembling like a paper-thin leaf faced with a hurricane. I'd never experienced one in my life, having lived in Northern Ireland, with its drizzly but moderate climes. But it felt like a fitting comparison. I was seeing my life and death stories merging, like they were coming together like diary entries once dispersed and then gathered in their proper order; only then could they begin to make sense.

I didn't have anything left to say for myself. Self-defence was utterly pointless when you knew someone know your transgressions and that there was no turning back. I wished I could beg for another opportunity to make it right, but I knew I didn't deserve it. I'd had so many opportunities to correct it on Earth, had I listened to the slightest twinges in my heart. But I was preoccupied. And preoccupation seemed to create awful actions.

I knew that my thoughts weren't private, standing on that stand, under the intense light. But they never had been - I just hadn't known that there was always someone listening in.

The judge instructed the jury to deliberate on what my sentence should be. It took what felt like days and I didn't feel like I could breathe the whole time. I knew that air didn't exist there like it had on Earth, but I still had the sensation of suffocating. While I awaited my trial, I'd held on to the physical sensations of the body. I wouldn't be freed from them then, I thought. Death wasn't the end of suffering. Maybe it was just the beginning of a more gruesome chapter – for those that had left something shameful behind them.

I wondered if I should raise the topic of my other sins. I wanted to confess them and relieve myself of the burden of them, but I knew I wouldn't get the chance to do that. The judge didn't want to hear about them. And that would have been self-serving anyway – handing them over in exchange for forgiveness.

The deliberation of the jury was unbearable. Ordinarily, I knew on Earth that the court went into recess to allow for that. But there was no such break there. No one else looked like they were aware of time. Maybe, I thought, that was something I'd held onto from my human experience because I hadn't properly crossed over yet. The chattering of the jury was loud, but I still couldn't make out a single word that they were saying. Finally, they went silent and waved to the judge. The judge had been sitting the whole time in a blissful silence – a kind of peace I would have given anything to obtain.

They spoke, in what sounded like tongues to the judge, and I could feel it listening intently to whatever they had to say. Then, the judge silenced everyone with an unspoken sign. I felt the urge to shut up too. I wouldn't have dared to express a word then, even if I'd been in immense pain. I awaited my sentence. It wasn't what I expected at all. My small mind could never have conceived of the creativity of the judge and his jury. Their eyes could see things I couldn't even perceive, and I was at their mercy. It was ironic that I'd thought so little of all the little lives at my mercy in my time on Earth, but I'd never considered lightening their sentence. It was strange to think that all the good deeds I'd thought I was doing had counted for nothing overall. You can think you're a good person, overall, and then find out that something you thought was a small misdeed weighed against you most of all.

"You demonstrated genuine remorse in your thoughts during the lessons served to you," said the judge.

Its voice sounded harsh, but it was only adapting to the circumstances with which it was dealing. I knew I'd been harsh in ways I had never even considered as important. I wondered how he'd ask me to correct them.

"I've decided on your sentence, with the help of the jury," he said.

He seemed to be able to understand what they were thinking and saying from across the room. I supposed that came with omniscience.

"You will forever be coloured by your actions. Your chance to undo them was in your lifetime. It might have been short, but you were given so many chances, and you never strayed from your path of cruelty. You had a religious upbringing, didn't you?"

"Yes, but it was a Christian one."

"Yes, but the basic principles were the same."

"Ok, but I didn't know about how things really were – there were no teachings on that. The Bible never specifically referred to insects and their importance."

"You're making excuses again for your actions," it said, notably disappointed. But it didn't seem angry with me – just patient in its disappointment with me. I wished things could have been different, but it was too late.

"You will serve the spider spirits."

"What are they?" I asked. I couldn't imagine anything worse. Despite the fact I'd been in the body of one and seen things from their perspective, my fear of them remained.

"The souls of the spiders that suffered on Earth. Your life will depend on their kindness, or lack thereof."

I could feel the sensation of crying coming over me, but when I touched my face, it was dry. I must have lost the ability to produce bodily fluids, but I still had the sensation of needing to. It wasn't how I'd pictured death being. I thought it was meant to be a release from the discomfort of living.

"I will grant you a kindness though – I know how much your parents mean to you, so you will get to see them."

That thought gave me a sliver of hope. I thought I could endure anything if I knew that that would be the reward. They were everything I had, and I had never attached as closely to anyone since that. It felt like an important loophole.

"Are they safe?" I asked.

"Yes, they are in paradise," said the judge.

I could tell it gave the judge some satisfaction to share that with me. It didn't want to see me in agony. I could sense that from the stand. It was a beautiful energy and I realised that that was what mattered – not whether I was happy or even comfortable. I was a speck on the enormous spiritual canvas, and I could self-sacrifice in order to bring fairness to other creatures. That was what made me feel happy and what gave me hope.

I felt a warmth spreading through my heart and I felt something change on the inside. I felt sorry for everything I'd done wrong in my life. I could see the extent of the damage I'd done, and it was extreme. I knew I was getting what I deserved and that seeing my parents would get me through every minute of it. I was so excited about seeing them.

The judge walked towards the door and commanded it to open. It filled with the strongest light I'd ever seen. It was definitely otherworldly, and I knew getting to see it was a privilege and a gift from the judge. Two forms moved through the light, and I saw the beaming faces of my parents.

"Betsy," they called me. They were calm but I could tell that they were as desperate to see me as I had been to see them. I wondered if Paradise could still be good when you were missing someone that hadn't made it there. We embraced each other and I felt safe for a long moment. It was like everything else evaporated away: all the errors made, and the disappointments caused. We were just part of a happy unit. I could feel the goodness coming from them and it filled me up with better energy too. The whole experience I'd had for however long I'd been there had left me drained and saddened by everything. The judge let them stay for a long time. I imagined it was what it felt when prisoners received visitation. I knew I had to leave afterwards, but I wanted to savour it while it lasted. I could have spoken to my parents and caught up on everything, but we just remained in comfortable silence. Sometimes a hug says more than a thousand explanatory words ever could.

Eventually, I knew it was time to go. I saw the shadow of the spider on the wall. It was approaching at a leisurely pace, like it didn't want to startle me. I pulled away from my parents and locked eyes with it. It didn't look angry when we made eye contact; it looked forgiving. And then, I was sure I saw it smile.

The End.

Never Swat a Fly

Printed in Great Britain
by Amazon